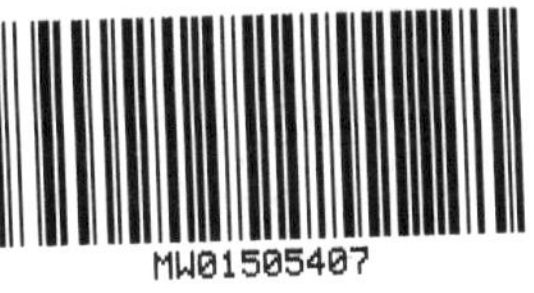

Praise for *Me and My Ghoulfriends* by Rose Pressey

"Rose Pressey spins a delightful tale with misfits and romance that makes me cheer loudly."
Coffee Time Romance

"Her characters are alive and full of quick-witted charm and will make you laugh. The plot twists keep you turning the pages non-stop."
Para Normal Romance

"I absolutely loved this book! It had me chuckling from the beginning."
Fallen Angel Reviews

CRIME WAVE

Rose Pressey's Complete Bookshelf

Maggie, P.I. Mystery Series:
Book 1 – Crime Wave
Book 2 – Murder is a Beach

The Halloween LaVeau Series:
Book 1 – Forever Charmed
Book 2 – Charmed Again
Book 3 – Third Time's a Charm

The Rylie Cruz Series:
Book 1 – How to Date a Werewolf
Book 2 – How to Date a Vampire
Book 3 – How to Date a Demon

The Larue Donovan Series:
Book 1 – Me and My Ghoulfriends
Book 2 – Ghouls Night Out
Book 3 – The Ghoul Next Door

The Mystic Café Series:
Book 1 – No Shoes, No Shirt, No Spells
Book 2 – Pies and Potions

The Veronica Mason Series:
Book 1 – Rock 'n' Roll is Undead

A Trash to Treasure Crafting Mystery:
Book 1 – Murder at Honeysuckle Hotel

The Haunted Renovation Mystery Series:
Book 1 – Flip that Haunted House
Book 2 – The Haunted Fixer Upper

Rose Pressey

Crime Wave

A Maggie, P.I. Mystery

Thomas & Mercer

This is a work of fiction. Names, characters, organizations, places, events, and incidents are either products of the author's imagination or are used fictitiously.

Published by Thomas & Mercer, Seattle

www.apub.com

ISBN-13: 9781477818190
ISBN-10: 1477818197
Library of Congress Control Number: 2013919652

Cover design by Inkd

Printed in the United States of America

This is to you and you know who you are.

Chapter One

When I was a kid, my mother ogled Tom Selleck every week during episodes of *Magnum P.I.*, gushing about his mustache or his manly chest and dazzling smile. Of course, at the time I hadn't understood what the fuss was about, but now I totally got why she was drooling. Watching reruns of *Charlie's Angels* and *Magnum, P.I.* had caused me to daydream about what it would be like to be a private investigator. I've been a fan of detective shows ever since and still watch the reruns to this day.

Not in my wildest dreams had I ever thought becoming a private investigator would be an option for me. Okay, I had daydreamed about it a lot, but I'd never thought it would become a reality. I'd given up any idea of working in law enforcement years ago when I changed my college major from criminal justice to fashion design.

But that all changed when my uncle had a heart attack and left me his faltering P.I. agency. His death had come as a total shock... Okay, it had been only a little bit of a surprise. Other than smoking and drinking, my uncle Griffin Thomas had been the picture of health.

Right before my move to Miami Beach, I'd decided to make a new start with everything in my life. I'd added caramel highlights to my dark hair and even bought a few new outfits. Nothing high fashion or anything... mostly just shorts and T-shirts to replace

the ones that had holes in them. I did, however, buy a daring red cocktail dress.

When I'd packed it in my suitcase, I'd wondered what the heck had come over me. What made me think I'd ever go anywhere wearing the thing? After all, it had been quite some time since I'd had a date. But a girl could dream, right?

Relationships seemed so complicated. I'd been dating a man for over a year when he'd broken up with me out of the blue. At the time, he'd said I was too nice ... too sweet for him and that I'd eventually break up with him anyway. He had gone for the preemptive breakup.

Later I'd found out it was really because he'd met someone new. I won't lie and say that it didn't hurt, but what could I do? Apparently, he wanted a woman who was a little less predictable and had more of a wild side. Now I'd show the world that I wasn't so predictable after all.

It had been difficult to make the move down to Miami. Finding a decent and cheap place to live had been especially hard. But I'd found a studio apartment after a couple days. So what if it was the size of a closet?

The place was only a couple blocks from the beach and a short drive to the office, so that made it bearable. I'd grown up on the other side of Florida in the Panhandle. When Uncle Griffin passed away and left me the agency, I threw my clothes in my Ford and made the drive down to Miami.

When I dressed this morning, I had a tough time deciding what a private investigator should wear to work. A trench coat and pipe were out of the question. Since my apartment was small, that meant the closet would barely hold a broom. My clothing space was limited, making my outfit options rather minuscule. There wasn't enough space to store a new wardrobe even if I had been able to afford one.

Anyway, my outfit needed to be comfortable in case I had to sit for an extended length of time on a stakeout. I knew the odds that I'd have a stakeout on the first day were unlikely, but I wanted to be prepared. I'd settled on a green blouse that brought out the green in my hazel eyes. Plus, green was my favorite color, not entirely because it highlighted the green in my eyes, but that didn't hurt either. Since the temperature outside was somewhere around "heat stroke," I wore long white shorts and sandals.

As I'd studied my reflection in the mirror hung over the closet door, I realized that my outfit didn't exactly scream private eye. But I was comfortable and that was the most important thing. I knew sandals wouldn't be good for a lot of walking or running, but I'd be sitting around all day, right? So what difference did it make?

So now I was sitting behind a cheap wooden desk on a metal chair that made my butt numb after about two minutes. Shifting in my seat, I tapped an ink pen against a yellow legal pad, contemplating my current situation. Uncle Griffin hadn't even owned a computer, for heaven's sake. Two metal file cabinets sat against the wall near the door. Apparently, that had been his sole means of organization.

The other day I'd ordered several items from the private investigator gadget website. I was excited about the prospect of using these new toys. I'd spent more money than I should have . . . definitely more than I could afford. But the items would pay for themselves in the long run, right? That was assuming I actually landed cases and completed them successfully.

To be honest, I'd purchased what the website called a "Private Investigator Kit." I would never admit that to anyone though. If asked, I'd deny it until the end. I mean, it sounded as if I'd purchased an Inspector Clouseau kit from the toy store. In reality, this kit was just some of the more popular items from the online store that were bundled together to save money. I love a good bargain.

I was most excited about using the digital recorder disguised as an ink pen and the video recorder sunglasses.

The office walls were painted an ugly pea-green color, and an old mini-refrigerator hummed loudly in the corner of the room. I shuddered just remembering what I'd found in there when I'd cleaned it out. To top it off, there was barely room to turn around in this space without cracking a knee on the desk. Trust me; I had the bruises to prove it.

The office had one redeeming quality, though. A breathtaking sliver of beach view was visible through the tiny window on the far left wall. If you leaned your head in just the right direction, you could catch a beautiful view. *Griffin Thomas, P.I.* was written across the tempered glass of the front door. As soon as I could afford it, I'd change it to read: *Maggie Thomas, P.I.*

Uncle Griffin had mainly advertised for cheating spouse cases or finding long-lost relatives. I was pretty sure he'd never tracked down any long-lost relatives, though. That would mean he'd actually had some success. After losing my job as a telemarketer, I couldn't be too picky about career choices. I mean, who gets fired from a telemarketing job? In my defense, no one really wanted to buy their own burial plot. Anyway, money was tight and the rent was due: I had to make this work.

Yes, for better or for worse, this place was now mine. Before arriving in town, I'd taken the time to get my concealed carry permit and private investigator license. I'd passed the test, but how prepared was I for the actual work? It was one thing to take a written exam, but an entirely different ball game to actually help a real client. Like I said, I'd studied criminal justice in college, but gave up on the thought that I'd actually ever use any of that experience.

To my surprise, there was already an appointment on my schedule for this morning. A man had called earlier, and with his rushed words, I knew he was in a hurry to meet with me. Uncle Griffin employed a woman who manned the phones and did whatever else

an assistant to a private eye was supposed to do. But Dorothy Raye had informed me that she wouldn't be in today until ten, so I was on my own until she got there. She mentioned something about picking up her new orthopedic shoes, but I hadn't really paid attention to the details.

When the knock rattled the door, a flood of emotion rushed through me. I would consider it a huge success if I made it through my first appointment without uttering something stupid or some equally embarrassing event happening.

Jumping up from my desk, I maneuvered around the tight space and opened the agency's front door. Unfortunately, the space was too small for a waiting room. The middle-aged man looked me up and down with a critical eye. He wore a tailored gray pinstriped suit. It wasn't the cheap material that my uncle's suits had been made out of, either. This thing was the real deal. The bright blue tie matched his eyes. His short hair had sprinkles of gray in the otherwise dark strands.

After an awkward pause, I said, "You must be Mr. Abbott. Won't you please come in?"

I stepped out of the way and gestured toward the small metal chair in front of the desk. Uncle Griffin had clearly pulled out all the stops to impress the clients. The chair looked more like a torture device to force someone to talk. Updating the office furniture was another thing to add to my to-do list, as soon as I could afford it, of course.

"Is Mr. Thomas available?" he asked as he walked briskly into the room.

There was no point in beating around the bush. "He's dead," I blurted out.

Mr. Abbott turned to me with a shocked expression. "He's dead?"

I moved around the desk and took a seat. "I'm sorry I didn't inform you on the phone when you made the appointment."

In hindsight, I should have divulged that little detail, but it makes for an awkward conversation, so I'd put it off as long as possible.

The chair creaked loudly as he sat down, and I prayed he wouldn't fall though the old thing. He clutched a manila envelope in his hand.

"Yes, you should have." His brows drew downward in a frown.

I cleared my voice and continued, "Yes, well, my name is Maggie Thomas. I've taken over the agency for my late uncle. I can assure you that you'll get the same level of professionalism and service with me."

Okay, I couldn't actually assure him of that, but what was I supposed to say? I couldn't tell him he was my first case ever. Perhaps if he gave me the case and it was successful, I could let him in on my little secret.

After another long pause, he said, "I'm in a bit of a hurry, so I trust you can work quickly on this."

I nodded. "Of course. What is it you want me to do?"

Mr. Abbott's expression darkened. I didn't like the look on his face. He had been extremely vague when I'd spoken to him on the phone. No matter how badly I needed the money, I refused to do anything illegal.

"I believe my wife is cheating on me, and I'd like for you to obtain the proof," he said matter-of-factly.

Oh, was that all? I could handle that. How hard could it be? I'd follow her to some hourly rate hotel, snap a few photos, and then get paid. But why the Thomas Agency? Mr. Abbott had told me on the phone that he was a partner at some big law firm. Surely he had some fancy, high-powered agency to use. No matter what the circumstances though, it was an easy job, and I was going to take it. My first real case.

"Don't you have a real, er, I mean, a regular private investigating agency that you use for your law firm?" I leaned forward in my chair.

"I'd rather keep this matter confidential. I'm sure you understand?" The line of his mouth tightened a fraction more.

I nodded. "Absolutely."

"I was told that Griffin Thomas was good." He folded his hands in his lap.

Who would have told him such a thing?

"Yes, he was the best," I said.

I had no idea if Uncle Griffin had been the best, but it sounded good anyway.

Mr. Abbott placed an envelope on the desk and scooted it toward me. "Enclosed is a photo of my wife and other essential information."

I stared down at the envelope for a moment, then finally picked it up. As I slid a manila folder out of the envelope, a photo fluttered to the floor. Mr. Abbott frowned, then reached down and picked up the picture, handing it to me. I took the photo from his outstretched hand, pretending not to notice his scowl. "Thank you."

The glossy photo featured a woman in her mid-fifties with shoulder-length blonde hair and big bright blue eyes. Her smile revealed perfect white teeth. She looked so sweet; she couldn't possibly cheat on him, right?

"She's very pretty," I said.

He scowled. "Yes, she is beautiful."

I opened the large file and spread the contents across my desk. The remaining papers in the file listed her address, height, weight, and favorite hangouts. He'd practically done my job for me already.

I met my client's gaze. "Mr. Abbott, what makes you think she's cheating on you?"

"Please, call me Arthur." His tone was terse, but surprisingly calm.

I nodded. "Okay, Arthur."

"My wife always claims that she is going to yoga class, but I know that she couldn't possibly stretch that much." His mouth deepened into an even deeper frown.

"Maybe she really needs the relaxation?" I attempted my best compassionate grin.

He scowled again. "No, I don't think so. What has she got to relax from? I make sure that she has everything she could possibly want."

Did he? Arthur Abbott was obviously an affluent man, but money couldn't buy everything, right? Regardless, it was none of my business. He was hiring me to do a job, not assess their personal relationship.

"Well, I'll see what I can find and will provide you with a full report . . . and any evidence that I may uncover." I leaned back in my chair.

Pushing to his feet, Arthur reached into his suit pocket and handed me his card. "I've written my address on the back of the card. My wife and I aren't living together at the moment. I have a condo that I'm staying at for now. You'll find the cash for your fee in the envelope."

I flipped the card over and looked at the address scribbled across the back. It was none of my business why he'd moved out, but nonetheless, I had to ask. "Why are you living apart? Is it because of her suspected infidelity?"

"We started arguing when I questioned her about being away so often. That's when I decided to move out for a while." He glanced at his gold watch.

"Do you have any idea who she's seeing?" I asked.

"No, but when I find the bastard—" He cut off his words before saying too much.

Finding the bastard definitely wasn't my job. All I had to do was provide Arthur with the evidence that his wife was cheating, not whom she was cheating with.

"Do you know what you'll do if I capture evidence?" Our eyes met for a moment, but he quickly looked away, checking his watch again.

Did he plan on divorcing her? What other reason would he have to check up on her if he didn't plan on divorce? I hoped he didn't plan to kill the man she might be sleeping with. I didn't want to be a part of a murder investigation.

Arthur paused with his hand on the door and turned to look at me. "I'll be waiting for your call."

With that, he walked out of my office. Obviously, he thought my last question didn't warrant an answer. Whatever. I had a case now and that was all that mattered. I hurried over to the window and watched as Arthur climbed into his Lexus and drove off.

I glanced at my watch. It was exactly ten a.m. Where was my assistant? The thought had barely floated from my mind when the front door opened wide. Dorothy rushed through with a giant white purse looped over her arm. We'd met only briefly since I'd arrived in Miami.

Her gray hair was pulled up high and pinned into a prim bun at the back of her head. Her orange tropical-print skirt reached to her ankles, drawing even more attention to her spiffy silver-sequined canvas sneakers. A white linen blouse finished off her ensemble. Dorothy had a spry gleam in her blue eyes, and the knobs of her cheeks were painted with bright pink blush.

"I'm here now." Dorothy waved her arm through the air as if all my troubles were now over.

I jumped up from my desk, grabbing the file. "Dorothy, I'm glad you're here. I have a case and I need to get started right away. You can stay and answer the phone for me, right?"

We both knew that the chances of someone calling were slim, but it could happen and I wanted to be as professional as possible.

Dorothy stopped in her tracks, placing her hands on her hips. She tilted her eyeglasses down on her little nose and her

mouth dropped open. Finally, after gawking at me for several seconds she said, "You got a job? But it's your first day."

"I know. Isn't it great? I mean, it's only a cheating spouse case, but hey, it'll help pay the bills around here." I waved the file through the air.

Uncle Griffin had left me a small amount of money to keep the business afloat until I could get on my feet, but that money was running out fast.

Her mouth twisted into a smile, and then she said, "Well, that's fabulous. You go ahead and I'll somehow manage the phones." She waved me off.

Okay, now she was just mocking me. Dorothy had worked for my Uncle Griffin for several years, but other than that, I didn't know much about her. In his will, he had insisted that she keep her job at the agency. In spite of her sometimes sarcastic tone, I liked her well enough.

I grabbed my purse and gun and headed for the door. "I'll have my cell phone if you need me."

"I'll make sure to call you, dear." She scoffed and waved me off again.

I was sure she just wanted me gone so she could get to her knitting. Who was she knitting for anyway? We lived in Miami, for heaven's sake. It was nine thousand degrees outside.

I headed out the door and toward my little red Ford Focus. The smell of sea tickled my nostrils, and a few hundred seagulls circled the area. Okay, maybe it wasn't a few hundred, but I was pretty sure the birds were plotting to dive-bomb my head at any moment. Visions of that Alfred Hitchcock movie flashed through my head. I hurried to my car and jumped in, dumping my purse onto the passenger seat and securing my gun in the glove compartment.

With the key in the ignition, I turned the engine, but nothing other than a loud cranking noise sounded. I tried again with the same result. Of all the damn times for my car to bite it. I hit the

steering wheel with my fists, but that only made matters worse because now my hands were aching.

I glanced out the window toward the sky and watched the birds as they continued to circle the area. What would I do now? Grabbing my gun and purse, I hopped out of the car and marched back to the office.

Chapter Two

Dorothy tossed her knitting needles on the floor and clutched her chest when I rushed through the door. "You scared the hell out of me."

"Sorry, the birds . . ." I gestured.

She shook her head and frowned. "I promised I wouldn't feed them anymore. As soon as they realize I'm not handing out food they'll go away."

I waved my hand. "Never mind that. I think my car battery is dead and I need to use your Cadillac."

Her eyes widened. "I'm sorry, Maggie, but no one drives my car but me."

I gaped at her. "Are you serious?"

She eased the knitting needles and yarn from the floor and stuffed them into her purse. "Dead serious."

I released a deep breath and ran my hand through my hair. This was not going as I'd envisioned it. "Okay, fine. You'll have to drive me, then."

"But who will answer the phones?" She pointed at the receiver with a smirk.

"Oh, let's be real. No one is going to call. I'll just forward all calls to my cell phone. Now grab your purse and let's go." I motioned over my shoulder.

Once inside her Cadillac, I had second thoughts about asking her to drive. Dorothy stood at about four foot ten. She had the seat pushed all the way to the front of the steering wheel and a huge pillow propped behind her back just so she could reach the gas pedal.

"So you decided to get a Cadillac, huh?" I glanced over my shoulder and watched as her car came dangerously close to mine, parked directly behind her.

Why had she gotten such a huge car?

"There's more metal to protect me in case of a crash," she offered.

I fastened my seat belt and said a silent prayer. Dorothy punched the gas and my head slammed back onto the headrest.

"Sorry about that. The pedal sticks sometimes," she said as she steered the big wheel.

"Not a problem," I said, rubbing my neck.

"Where are we headed?" she asked as she pulled out onto the highway.

I opened up the file and searched the page for Allison Abbott's home address. According to Arthur's notes, she would be leaving for a yoga class soon. Or at least that was what she'd told him she was doing. If things went my way, I'd soon find out the truth.

"We need to head over to Thirty-Sixth Street," I said.

Dorothy cut the wheel and I clutched the side of the door.

She huffed. "Well, a little warning, dear, and I wouldn't have to make such an abrupt turn."

"Why are you driving so fast?" I asked.

"I'm not driving fast. Everyone else is driving too slowly," she said.

I glanced at my watch. "Well, as long as we don't hit any traffic, I don't think we need to be in that much of a hurry."

She shrugged her shoulders. "Whatever you say."

As soon as I was done for the day, I had to get the battery replaced in my car. There was no way I would ever ride with Dorothy again.

"So who is this woman?" she asked as she whizzed through the streets of downtown Miami.

For a moment I thought about keeping the information confidential, but I figured Dorothy would just snoop in the files anyway, so I might as well save her the trouble.

"Her name is Allison Abbott. She's married to Arthur Abbott. He's a partner at some major law firm here," I said.

"Oh yes, I've heard of them. They have those huge billboards all over town. Ambulance chasers." She waved her hands through the air and the car swerved.

I grabbed the wheel just in time before she took out a side mirror on a parked car.

I shrugged. "I wouldn't know. I didn't ask and it's really none of my business."

"So she is cheating on him?" She tut-tutted. "That's a shame. I wonder who she's cheating with."

"I guess we'll find out." I said, studying the papers and trying not to look up. The less I saw of her driving, the better off I'd be.

"How do you plan on catching her?" she asked.

"We'll follow her," I said.

"You mean I have to tail someone?" Panic sounded in Dorothy's voice.

"You should have let me drive your car."

Dorothy patted the steering wheel. "Like I said, no one drives this baby."

After giving directions to Dorothy, I tried to collect my thoughts. Coming up with a game plan would be essential to the successful outcome of this case. In spite of my best attempts, though, my thoughts were continually interrupted by either Dorothy's less-than-stellar driving or her rapid succession of questions.

"Just don't get yourself into trouble. I was constantly warning Griffin, but unfortunately it was the fried foods that got him." She shook her head.

"Well, I don't like fried foods and I promise not to get into trouble," I said.

"You say that now . . ." She wagged her finger.

As we drove down Biscayne Boulevard, I glanced over at Dorothy. She had both hands on the steering wheel and a dangerous gleam in her eyes. I didn't know much about Dorothy other than that she liked to feed the birds and knit, and that she was a terrible driver.

"Do you have any children, Dorothy?" I asked.

"I have a son who lives in New York. He comes to see me a couple times a year," she said with a smile.

"Oh, that's nice. What about a husband?" I asked.

She shook her head and kept her gaze focused on the road, which was a good thing. "He died about ten years ago. It's just me now. I have my Bunco friends, though."

I smiled softly. "That's nice."

"You should play Bunco with us sometime." Her face lit with a bright smile.

I nodded, even though I had no idea what Bunco was.

"That's the street right there," I said, pointing to the road up ahead.

Elegant homes lined the street. Palm trees flanked the pebble driveways and the sprinklers made the vegetation glisten.

As I counted down the house numbers, I said, "The house is the fifth one down on the right. We should stop a couple houses ahead of that and just park on the road."

"Won't she see us waiting for her?" Dorothy asked.

"Well, I can't exactly conceal your Cadillac behind a palm tree, now, can I?" I retorted.

She wiggled her finger at me. "Don't sass me. You're just like your Uncle Griffin, always with the sassy tongue."

"I'm sorry," I said softly.

"That's all right. But don't let it happen again."

I tapped my fingers against the file folder and contemplated my next move. "We'll have to sit here until she comes out. When she pulls out, wait a little bit, and then follow her."

"What if she knows we're following her?" Dorothy asked.

"I won't even entertain that thought. We'll just hope for the best." I crossed my fingers.

"What kind of car are we looking for?" Dorothy adjusted her eyeglasses.

"A black Mercedes."

"Oh, fancy." She wiggled her eyebrows.

"The gate's opening," I whispered.

She lowered her voice in return. "Why are you whispering?"

I chuckled. "I have no idea." I pointed toward the driveway as the sleek black Mercedes pulled out onto the street. "There she is. Once she starts down the road, pull out, but keep a few car lengths back. We don't want her to figure out what's going on."

Dorothy gave a little salute, then cranked the engine and put the car into drive. After a few seconds, she pulled out. My heart rate increased as adrenaline pumped through my body.

"You're not so bad at this private eye stuff after all," I said with a smile.

Dorothy had both hands tightly on the steering wheel. "We'll see about that."

She navigated the big car out onto Biscayne Boulevard again, keeping a safe distance from the Mercedes. So far, so good. The yoga studio that Arthur said his wife went to in the mornings was only a couple of miles away and we were nearing the street where we'd soon turn.

"She's turning," I said.

Dorothy swung the wheel hard to the left and I slid in the seat. "Hold on" she said.

I blew the hair out of my eyes and straightened my body in the seat. "For the love of knitting, will you slow down?"

As we sped down the road, trying to keep our distance, I searched the addresses on the buildings. When we reached the building with *Yoga Studio* written on the window, Allison Abbott kept driving.

"She passed the place up. I wonder if she knows we're following her," I said.

"Well, if she looked in her rearview mirror at all, she probably figured it out." Dorothy's voice had a sigh in it.

Yeah, she probably thought a grandmother was stalking her. Now that I thought of it, Dorothy might be a good way to throw people off our tracks. I'd have to remember that for the future.

"Keep following her and see where she goes." I pointed.

"How long do we follow her?" she asked.

"Until one of us runs out of gas, I guess." I glanced over at the gas gauge and saw that it was on full.

Filling the tank up before I took off on a stakeout wasn't something I'd thought about until now. If I ran out of gas, the end result would be disastrous. I'd have to be more careful in the future.

"Don't you worry. I always keep gas in my car. I never want to be stranded. When it gets on half full, I drive her right to the gas station." She gestured, taking her hand off the wheel momentarily.

After traveling a few more blocks, Allison turned the Mercedes into a pink Art Deco hotel parking lot. A blinking neon sign flashed *Vacancy* under the words *The Seagull Inn*. The parking lot was mostly empty, which was a bad thing for us. Most people didn't need a room in the middle of the day on a Tuesday, unless of course they were just meeting during their lunch break like these two lovebirds, Allison Abbott and the mystery man.

"It looks like you just got your answer," Dorothy said.

The adrenaline was really pumping now. It looked as if Arthur Abbott was correct about his wife. Now it was up to me to provide him with the proof.

"I have to get proof or it means nothing. Turn into the hotel and let's see what she does now," I said.

Dorothy wheeled the Cadillac into the hotel parking lot. "She sure didn't worry about finding the nicest hotel in town, did she? Where do we go now?"

"Park the car between that white truck and the red car." I pointed toward the vehicles at the back of the lot.

Allison had parked her car in front of room twelve. She opened the door and climbed out from behind the wheel. She was wearing a short white dress and wedge espadrille heels, definitely not yoga class apparel. She had a small clutch purse under her arm, but no overnight bag. It looked as if she wasn't planning on staying long.

I held my breath, waiting for her to turn her attention to us, but she never looked our way. If she knew we were there, she certainly didn't let on to the fact. How was I possibly going to get evidence that she was cheating? I wouldn't be able to see what was going on behind closed doors. This whole thing was kind of creepy when you thought about it—spying on people in their most intimate moments.

As she hurried over to the door, I pulled out my phone and readied it to snap pictures. My stomach was in knots waiting to see who would answer the door. Seconds after she knocked, a man with salt-and-pepper hair opened the door. He wore dark-colored slacks and a blue polo shirt. They immediately embraced in a kiss. It was the shot that I had been waiting for.

I snapped a rapid succession of photos. Then when they finally released their embrace, I snapped another few pictures of the man and then one of Allison's face as she turned around and glanced out over the parking lot. *Now* she was worried about someone watching her? She'd already kissed him. It was too late. This would have to be enough evidence for her husband because there was no way I would snoop around their window and try to get a more detailed photo of their indoor activities.

Dorothy started the car and shoved it into drive.

"What are you doing?" I asked.

"You got your pictures; now we can leave." She smiled.

"No, we can't leave yet. I have to wait until they're done. Or they come out. Whatever you want to call it," I said.

She frowned. "I'd rather not call it anything. They could be in there for a long time."

I smirked. "I'm guessing it won't take that long."

"He's a middle-aged man. They pop those Viagra pills like candy. We could be here for hours." She shook her head.

I hadn't thought of that and now I had a mental picture that I'd been trying to avoid all morning.

"Well, regardless of how long their encounter lasts, I have to wait," I said.

"I'm getting overtime for this," she warned with a wave of her index finger.

I pulled out my binoculars and focused them on the hotel room. What I was looking for, I had no idea. I'd already gotten pictures, but nonetheless, it seemed like what any private investigator was supposed to do. Dorothy had been right, even though I hadn't wanted to admit it. There was no telling how long we'd have to wait. This was the least glamorous part of my new job. I was still waiting for the glamorous part to show up. We might as well make ourselves comfortable, I figured. I'd have to remember to carry snacks for my next stakeout.

A clacking noise grabbed my attention and I whipped around to look at Dorothy. She was moving her knitting needles at a frantic pace.

"What in the heck are you doing?" I asked.

"What does it look like I'm doing? I'm knitting. I always do this when I'm bored or nervous." She continued clacking the needles together.

"So which is it now? Bored or nervous?"

She leaned her head down and peered at me over the top of her eyeglasses. "Both."

"We're supposed to be watching the building and its surroundings." I pointed at the hotel.

"Do you think they'll slip out the back window?" she said with a chuckle.

"As a matter of fact, that could happen. I have to be prepared. I'm a professional," I said, forcing confidence into my voice.

She released a heavy sigh and placed the needles back in her purse. "There. Are you happy now?"

"Thank you."

About twenty minutes passed and we sat in silence. Well, except for the sound of Dorothy anxiously tapping her fingers against the steering wheel. My arms were tired from holding up the binoculars. I took a break every few minutes, but I'd have to work out at the gym and build up my arm strength.

A soft rattling noise came from the driver's seat. I cast a glance at Dorothy. This time she'd removed the contents of her purse and was digging around at the bottom like she was searching for a trunk of gold.

I shook my head. "What are you doing now?"

She whipped a small candy out from the pits of her purse. "Would you like a peppermint, dear?"

I stared for a couple seconds, then reached out and took the candy from her hand. "Thank you."

How deep was the abyss of her purse?

"What do you have in there?" I leaned over and tried to peer in.

"Whatever you need, I got it," she said with a wave of her hand.

When I turned back around, Allison had already emerged from the hotel room. She was climbing into her car. I was torn about which move I should make next. I wanted to see the man leave the room and find out which car he got into, but I wondered where Allison would go next, too.

Since I'd already caught Allison in the act of adultery, I felt that it was more important to try and discover the identity of the mystery man. With a photo of him and description of his car, surely Arthur would know who this man was.

"We'll wait here and see who comes out of the room," I said.

"Don't you want to follow her?" Dorothy asked.

I shook my head. "I've already got what I need from her."

Dorothy shrugged. "It's your case to screw up."

I scowled. "I know what I'm doing."

Okay, I didn't really know, but I was doing my best. Catching Allison in the act had been exceptionally easy, though. Couldn't Arthur have followed her today just as I had? I'd gotten the evidence so easily that it almost seemed too good to be true. I'd take what I could get, though.

After a couple seconds, the man stepped out from the room. He glanced to his left and then to his right. Was he looking for someone? His big mistake was that he never once looked straight ahead out across the parking lot. If he had, he might have seen us. He pulled out his cell phone and dialed a number. As he talked on the phone he walked over and climbed behind the wheel of a silver Lexus.

"Get ready to follow him," I said.

"Oh, dear. I'm not cut out for this spy stuff," Dorothy said, stuffing a crossword puzzle book back into her giant purse.

"Okay, pull out now." I motioned as the man turned out onto the street.

Where was he going? As long as he didn't catch on that we were following him, we'd soon find out more about this mystery man. After a couple blocks, he turned left. Dorothy had somehow allowed a black SUV to get in between our car and the Lexus.

"These darn old drivers," she huffed.

Dorothy punched the gas and whipped around the SUV, flashing the old man the stink eye in the process. I held on tightly to the leather seat, probably leaving indents from my fingernails.

"He's getting onto the highway," I said.

"Oh, no, no. I don't do highways. People drive too fast." She shook her head.

"You've got to be kidding me. You passed that old guy back there like he was sitting still. I haven't seen anyone drive this fast since I went to that NASCAR race with my ex-boyfriend," I said.

She glanced over. "You're exaggerating, dear."

"Dorothy, you have to do this for me. After all, you wouldn't let me drive your car. Uncle Griffin would have wanted you to." I batted my eyelashes.

She released a heavy sigh. "Why did you have to bring his name into this? Just this once, but don't blame me if we get into an accident."

Something told me she wasn't joking. I said a silent prayer as she merged onto the busy highway. What did I have to lose at this point? After a couple of honking horns and a few more glares from Dorothy, she'd caught up with the Lexus. We trailed behind just enough that with any luck he wouldn't be suspicious.

Another couple of miles and he exited the highway.

"Good job, Dorothy," I said as she followed at a nice pace behind.

"I can do anything when I set my mind to it." She tapped her fingers against the steering wheel.

My stomach flipped as the Lexus sped up and zipped in and out of traffic.

"I think he may be on to us," Dorothy said as she struggled to keep up.

I knew he was really speeding if even she couldn't match his pace.

When we finally spotted his car again, he was turning into the parking lot of a small office building.

"Hurry before he gets out of the car and we can't see which building he goes into," I said.

"First you tell me to slow down and now you tell me to hurry up. Make up your mind, will you?" Dorothy said.

When we pulled into the parking lot, I spotted the sign on the outside of the building and couldn't believe my eyes. What was going on? The sign on the front read Abbott, Louis, and Cooper, PLLC. That was when it hit me that this was the address on Arthur Abbott's business card. Who was this man walking into Arthur's building? Was he possibly going inside to confront the husband of his lover?

"Where should I park?" Dorothy asked, snapping me out of my jumbled thoughts.

"Just pull into this spot right here. I have to call my client." I pointed.

She frowned, but didn't ask what was happening. I knew she'd get the full details soon enough. I dialed the number on the card that was listed for his office. If this man was really going to confront Arthur Abbott, then this scene could turn ugly quickly. What had I dragged my assistant into?

A woman answered the phone. "Abbott, Louis, and Cooper. How may I help you?"

"May I speak with Arthur Abbott?" My words were rushed.

She must have picked up on my panic. "I'm sorry, but he's not in the office right now. Is there anything I can help you with?"

Well, that was a bit of a relief. At least the men wouldn't get into a fight. Not right now, at least.

"Um, no, I guess not. Do you happen to know where he is?" I asked.

"I'm sorry. I can't give out that information. I can take your number and have him call you as soon as possible," she said in her best professional tone.

She sounded as if she'd dealt with her share of frantic people over the telephone.

"That's all right. Thank you anyway," I said, hanging up the phone without giving her a chance to say anything else.

How would I find out who this man was?

"What's going on now?" Dorothy asked.

I knew by the look in her eyes that she was about to whip out the knitting needles again if I didn't do something quickly. That was when it hit me. I could send Dorothy into the law firm to see who the man was. I mulled that plan over in my head for a couple seconds, then realized that I was nuts for even having the thought in the first place. I couldn't guarantee that she wouldn't go in there and totally give our cover away. Besides, I couldn't send someone else in to do my job. If I wanted to know who this man was, then I'd have to go inside the building myself.

"I have to go inside and find out who that man is. He went into the building where my client works. The law firm . . ." I pointed at the sign.

Dorothy pushed her eyeglasses up on her nose and peered for a few seconds. "I suppose it is. Huh. What do you make of that?"

"I don't know, but I intend to find out. Obviously, the man who is cheating with Allison Abbott knows that her husband works there. Maybe he came to confront him. I'm going in there to find out," I said.

A worried look crossed her face. "Just be careful."

"It's my job," I said with a half-hearted smile.

Chapter Three

When I stepped into the building, a blast of cold air hit me from the air conditioning. The lobby looked like any other, with nondescript fake leather chairs and a few old magazines stacked neatly on the coffee table in the middle of the room. I felt eyes on me and looked to my left. A blonde middle-aged woman stared at me, offering a strained smile.

"May I help you?" she asked.

I recognized her voice from the phone. It was at this point I realized I didn't have a plan. Was I going to ask "Who was the man who just entered?"

Finally I settled on, "I'm here to see Mr. Abbott."

She frowned, probably because she recognized my voice. "He's not here right now."

Footsteps to my right caught my attention. I glanced over and immediately panicked. I had "guilty" written all over my face. The mystery man whom Allison Abbott had been with at the hotel and whom I'd followed here was approaching me. What would I say to this man? He had to know that I followed him. He was coming over to confront me.

"Is everything okay, Ms. Smith?" he asked while looking at me.

The woman cast another glare my way, then said, "Yes, this lady is here to see Mr. Abbott. I told her he isn't in right now."

He knew this woman?

He held out his hand. “My name is Sam Louis. May I help you with something?”

I glanced over at the desk and saw his card lined up in the little holder beside the one for Arthur Abbott and another man named Matt Cooper. No wonder Arthur had hired me instead of using someone associated with the firm. Did Arthur suspect his partner of cheating with his wife?

I shook his hand, but I was sure my mouth was hanging open the entire time. I needed to get hold of myself.

“Um. No, I’ll just come back some other time. Thank you very much.” I turned and rushed out the door without looking back.

Sam Louis was the *Louis* in Abbott, Louis, and Cooper. He worked with Arthur and was cheating with Arthur’s wife. What a dirty rat. When I told Arthur about this I was sure it would turn his whole world upside down. I wasn’t looking forward to being the one to deliver that news. But had he already suspected what had been happening? If so, he hadn’t shared that bit of info with me.

When I climbed into the car, Dorothy asked, “What happened?”

“The mystery man is partners with my client. He’s cheating with his partner’s wife,” I said breathlessly.

“What a low-down, rotten thing to do.” Dorothy shook her head.

“We have to tell my client what I found out. We’ll go to his place.” I pointed toward the street. “Punch it, Dorothy!”

Chapter Four

When we pulled up to the building, I hopped out. "Do you want to come with me?" I felt bad that Dorothy had to sit in the car again.

She shook her head. "No, thank you. I'm doing just fine staying out of trouble here in the car. Besides, I'm getting paid overtime, right?"

She pulled out her knitting needles and flashed me a smile.

I scowled. "Yes, I guess you are."

The parking lot for the tower of condos was empty, which I found completely weird. Sure, it was the middle of the day and most people were at work, but I expected to see at least a few cars. There was one car parked at the first handicapped parking space next to the door. Arthur Abbott's Lexus. He wasn't supposed to park in that space. It was reserved for a disabled driver, but I guessed I'd let it slide since every other available spot was still available. It still wasn't an excuse as far as I was concerned, though.

I made my way through the glass entry doors and looked around. The lobby was empty and dark. The lights weren't even on. Had someone forgotten to pay the power bill? The elevators were down the hall a little and to the left. The dimly lit space was creepy and I looked around for another living soul, but found no one. I pushed the Up button for the elevator and the door

immediately opened. After a brief pause, I stepped forward and into the small box that dangled in the air on flimsy cables. Yeah, I was no fan of elevators.

From out of the shadowy hallway, a man appeared. He wore white pants and a blue shirt.

I clutched my chest. "You startled me."

He frowned. "May I help you?"

"I'm just here to see Arthur Abbott." I looked at the card Arthur had given me. "He's in 1064."

The man glared at me as if I'd just said the most offensive thing possible, then turned and walked out the door. That was odd. What had that been about?

I took the elevator up to the tenth floor and tried not to think about how much I hated heights. When the door chimed and opened, I let out the deep breath I'd been holding. I hurried off the elevator and down the hallway, looking at the numbers on the doors. This place was like a ghost town. Why was no one around? It was odd, almost as if the building had been abandoned. Was there a hurricane evacuation and no one had told me about it?

When I reached the door marked 1064, I knocked. I glanced over and spotted a doorbell, so I pushed on it a couple times. No one was answering. As I stood there, I took out my cell phone and dialed, praying that Arthur Abbott would pick up the phone this time. Again, he didn't pick up, but in the distance I heard a phone ringing. That must be his cell phone, right? Where had he taken off to?

When I knocked on the door again, it rattled. It looked as if someone had tampered with the door. The frame had been pulled away from the door slightly. My heart rate increased. I turned the knob, and to my surprise, the door was unlocked. So what if he didn't answer the door and it looked as if someone had broken in? I had to be brave and check out the place.

I opened the door slightly and called out, "Mr. Abbott, it's Maggie Thomas. Are you home?"

When no answer came, I squared my shoulders and stepped into the room. The entire wall at the rear of the room was glass, overlooking the Atlantic Ocean. The bright blue water and white sand were breathtaking. Quiet engulfed the condo. There was no television playing, no talking, and no radio. Maybe he'd had a problem with the door and had gone to find someone to replace it. Everything seemed to be in place, so I figured no one had broken in to steal anything. Shades of white with sprinkles of blue dominated the décor. The whole building being empty gave me the creeps. It was like the apocalypse had taken place and I was the only one left. It was just me and the little lizard that I spotted crawling on the balcony outside the glass doors.

I stepped across the room and stopped in front of the floor-to-ceiling window. I placed my hand on the glass and peered down. People dotted the beach below, but the condo's pool was empty. Not just devoid of people, but it had no water in it, reinforcing my idea that this place looked abandoned. What was that all about? I'd have to ask Arthur when I found him.

To my right was a glass sculpture. I wasn't sure of its significance, but it was pretty nonetheless. I picked up the art and studied it for a second before placing it back on the table.

That was when I spotted an arm on the floor. At least that was all I could see and I assumed that a body was attached to that arm. I prayed that a body was attached.

I hurried over to the beige-colored leather sofa. "Mr. Abbott, are you okay?"

I nudged his body with my foot, but he didn't move. It sure didn't look as if he was okay considering that there was a large amount of blood staining the white rug underneath his body. I glanced around the room to see if we were alone. I didn't want to be in here if there

was a killer still around. Had Arthur taken his own life, or had someone taken it for him? No one appeared to be in the condo, but they could have been hiding in another room waiting to attack me. I had to get out of there and dial 911. I reached down and checked for a pulse, but found none. Well, I hadn't seen this turn of events happening.

As I rushed out the door, I called the police. My thoughts raced as I took the elevator down to wait for them to show up.

Dorothy looked up from her knitting when I ran out the front door of the building.

Her eyes widened when I approached the car. "What in the name of heaven is wrong with you?"

"My client is dead," I said breathlessly.

"You killed your client?" she screeched.

"No! I didn't kill my client. He was dead when I got there," I said with panic in my voice.

"What happened to him?" she asked.

"I don't know, but the police are on their way." I ran my hand through my hair and released a deep breath.

Dorothy and I sat in silence while we waited for the police. Finally, sirens sounded announcing their arrival. When they approached, I pointed toward the building and told them in which room they'd find Arthur's body.

A few minutes passed as Dorothy and I watched the activity. Soon I felt eyes on me. When I looked to my right, I saw a dark-haired man wearing a white shirt, blue tie, and dark pants walking straight toward me. He removed his aviator sunglasses and fixed his gaze on me. A gun was secured in its holster at his hip and I knew right away that he was with the police force.

"You found the body?" the police detective asked.

His dark eyes stared at me, not letting me go from their mesmerizing hold. I pulled the pink leather card case from my purse, pulled out a pink card, and handed it to him.

"I'm Maggie Thomas, Private Investigator."

He stared at it for a moment, as if he was memorizing every detail. Maybe I was imagining things, but I could have sworn the slightest of smiles crossed his lips. What was so funny?

"You found the body in the condo?" he asked again.

I swallowed hard, then replied, "Yes, that's right."

I wouldn't let him intimidate me. I knew my rights.

"Why were you here?" He tapped the edge of my business card with his finger.

"He's my client," I said, trying to sound confident.

"And what was the nature of the case?" he asked in his professional tone.

I paused, wondering if I should tell him or not, but then I figured they might arrest me for murder, so I decided to spill my guts.

"He believed his wife was cheating on him. I followed her today and confirmed that was true. When I followed the man she's cheating with, he went to the deceased's law firm. Arthur Abbott is a lawyer, you know. Or he was a lawyer," I said, letting out a pent-up breath.

The detective gave me that same look again. The look that said *Aw, aren't you cute, trying to play detective.*

"Go on," the detective urged.

"Anyway, I followed the man inside the office and that was when I realized that he's Arthur Abbott's partner in the law firm." I rushed my words.

"Is that right?" the detective eyed me up and down.

I didn't back down from his stare. Two could play that game.

After what felt like forever, he said, "We'll need you to give a full statement, if you don't mind."

I straightened. "Not at all."

"My name is Detective Jackson, by the way." He soaked up my appearance with his intense blue eyes.

"It's nice to meet you," I said.

He handed me his business card. “You can call me Jake if you’d like.”

I peeked at the card quickly. Jake. I liked that name. But it was odd ... why was he being so informal with me? He didn’t know me.

“Did you touch the body?” He stared, waiting for my answer.

It depended on his definition of touching the body. Poking it with my foot? Checking for a pulse? Hmm. I supposed all of those things constituted touching the body.

“Yes, I checked to see if he had a pulse,” I answered reluctantly.

He frowned.

I threw my hands up. “Well, what did you want me to do? I had to see if he was still alive, right?”

“Did you touch anything else in the condo?” he asked without answering my previous question.

“Other than the doorknob, the window by the dining room, the sofa, the figurine in the dining room, and the coffee table, no, I didn’t touch anything.” I counted each one off on my fingers.

He closed his eyes for a moment, then finally said, “I thought you were a private investigator. Don’t you know you’re not supposed to touch those things?”

I knew all too well that I’d failed at Private Investigator 101. It was too late to worry about it now, though. What was done was done. I liked to think of it as learning as I went. As long as I stayed out of prison in the process, I’d be good.

“Of course I know I’m not supposed to touch things at a murder scene, but I didn’t know he was dead, therefore I didn’t know that it was a murder scene, now, did I?” I smirked.

The corners of his mouth turned up into a slight grin. “No, I suppose you didn’t.”

I crossed my arms in front of my chest. “I’ve been thinking ... which I had plenty of time to do while waiting for you all to show up.”

He mimicked my actions and folded his arms in front of his muscular chest. "Please do continue."

"I think Mr. Abbott knew his attacker." I fixed my stare on his handsome face.

"Is that right? And what makes you think that?" The corners of his mouth turned up a bit more.

"Well, I figure based on the position of the body, it looks as if Mr. Abbott was sitting on the sofa. Someone obviously struck him and he fell forward onto the floor. He had a drink on the coffee table. I bet there was another drink on that table too. He was probably having a conversation with someone. I bet the killer took his drink with him when he left," I said with satisfaction.

He rubbed his chin with his hand. "Interesting detective work. What makes you think it was a male?"

Well, the fact that his law firm partner was cheating with Arthur's wife?

I shrugged. "I don't know, I just said *he*."

"You seem to have an intimate knowledge of what happened at the crime scene. Especially since we don't even know how the deceased died yet. It could be suicide; we just don't know yet." He looked at me suspiciously.

I waved my hand dismissively. "Oh, he didn't kill himself."

He raised an eyebrow. "He didn't?"

Okay, with every word that slipped out of my big mouth I was implicating myself. Soon enough I'd be staring at the backside of the bars in the Dade County jail.

"He didn't seem depressed is what I meant to say," I offered.

"Did you know him well?" he asked.

"Well, no, but he just hired me to investigate a case. And why would he kill himself right after that?" I pointed with my index finger. "I can answer that for you: he wouldn't."

Jake rubbed the back of his neck. "You said you found proof that his wife was cheating. Maybe he discovered that before you

had a chance to share with him what you'd found. Maybe that would have caused him to take his own life."

Well, damn. He did have a point, but still, I just had a feeling that it hadn't gone down like that.

"I suppose you could assume that was a possibility, but I just don't think he was the type to commit suicide." I shook my head.

"Thank you for your insight, Ms. Thomas." He nodded. "I'll be in touch."

A rush of adrenaline ran through me when he said that, but I wasn't sure why. What had Uncle Griffin gotten me into? I'd had a much easier time as a telemarketer.

Chapter Five

After speaking with another officer and giving him my full statement, I was allowed to leave.

I hurried over to the Cadillac and climbed in. “Let’s get out of here, Dorothy,” I said.

“I thought they’d never let you go,” Dorothy said as she turned the ignition and punched the gas pedal.

I waved my hand. “Well, they had no choice but to let me go. I did nothing wrong … other than finding the body.”

“That is bad luck, but there was one bright side.” Dorothy grinned.

“What’s that?” I asked curiously.

“That was a handsome man you were speaking with … a tall glass of water.” She wiggled her eyebrows. “What did he want?”

“He’s a detective and he was basically interrogating me, so I could care less how handsome he is. As a matter of fact, he was kind of rude,” I said.

“What did he do that was so rude?”

“He clearly didn’t think my private investigation skills were all that great. You should have seen the way he looked at my business card.”

She snorted.

I waved my finger in her direction. “Dorothy, don’t you make fun of me. It’s been a long day and I still don’t have a car that runs.”

"Don't you get sassy with me, young lady. I didn't take that sassiness from your uncle and I won't take it from you, either. As a matter of fact, this job is nothing but a headache. Why, if it wasn't for promising your uncle that I'd watch over you, I would be on the beach right now watching the shirtless hot guys in their swim trunks." She gestured toward the water and drove me back to the office.

After another two hours, my car battery had been replaced and I was headed home, fantasizing about soaking under a hot shower. I needed to wash off the day's stress and relax the tension churning inside me. When I walked through the door, I set my purse and gun on the table, then tossed my keys down and locked the door behind me. Sand littered the floor where I'd kicked off my shoes. The tiny space had a beige tile floor and beige walls—not exactly the most exciting colors. There was just enough room for a bed and a small desk. With my dwindling checking account, though, it would have to do until I could afford better. I'd brought my soft cream-colored floral comforter and added flowers in a vase to brighten up the room. It added a nice romantic touch without the actual romance. I'd have to have a date in order to have romance.

I turned up the air conditioner, but it sputtered in protest. Calling the landlord to repair the unit would do little good. He'd fixed the leaking pipe with duct tape. There was no way I wanted to find out how he'd repair the AC. I gave the unit a kick, then, when the pain set in, remembered that I was wearing flip-flops.

After a long shower, I collapsed onto my sofa with chocolate and reruns of *Magnum, P.I.* A couple hours passed and I flicked off the DVR with my remote. I'd seen this episode about fifty times, but it always made me nervous at the end when Thomas Magnum

found himself in such a troubling situation. Suddenly, I could totally relate to his plight.

The next morning, I was back in my office looking at the photos of Allison Abbott and Sam Louis. I wondered what Allison had thought when she'd found out her husband had been murdered? What had Sam Louis thought? And to think I'd just seen them before Arthur was murdered. Could they have been responsible for Arthur's death?

Dorothy hadn't arrived yet. She said she needed a leisurely morning to relax after what had happened the day before. I couldn't blame her for that. I'd told her she could take the whole day off, but she said that wouldn't be necessary. But to be honest, she could knit and solve crossword puzzles here just as easily as she could at home.

A knock sounded at the door and I jumped. I glanced around as if I expected someone else to answer the door, but I was the only one there, so it was totally up to me. I eased up from my chair and around the desk.

With my hand on the doorknob, I paused, then opened the door. The wind was knocked out of my chest when I saw who was standing in front of me. It was Allison Abbott. She wore jeans and a pink T-shirt that looked as if she'd slept in it. Today she had no makeup on and it looked as if she hadn't brushed her hair. I was at a loss for words.

"I guess you're surprised to see me here. May I come in?" She gestured with a tilt of her head.

There was no way I could refuse her. I had to know what she wanted. How did she know to come here? How had she found out about me? I stepped to the side, allowing her to enter the room.

"Please come in." I waved my hand through the air.

"Thank you," she said as she walked past me.

"How can I help you?" I asked.

Since I didn't know what else to say, I figured that was as good a place to start as any.

"I know you know who I am," she said, staring me straight in the eyes.

I nodded. "Yes, I do. Would you like to sit down?"

She eased down on the chair and placed her hands in her lap. It was hard to believe that just twenty-four hours ago her husband had been in the same place.

"I came here for a specific reason. My husband had your business card and I know why."

Chapter Six

"So you know why your husband had my card in his possession?"

She looked me right in the eyes and said, "He had it because he thought I was cheating on him and wanted you to catch me in the act."

"You knew that he was having someone follow you?" I asked just to confirm.

"No, I didn't know at first, not until I found your business card. That's when I put two and two together. He used another agency for anything work related, so I was always on the lookout for those guys. How did I let my guard down so easily? How did I allow you to follow me?" She put her head in her hands.

I shook my head. "I can't answer that question."

"Did you get proof of my affair?" She straightened in the chair, regaining her composure.

"I can't answer that question either," I said.

Although I wasn't sure why I couldn't answer. After all, my client was dead. He wouldn't know, but it seemed like the right thing to do.

She frowned. "I'll take that as yes. I won't even try to hide from you the fact that I was cheating with Sam Louis. But it's not like it seems."

"Cheating isn't like it seems?" I asked with a raised eyebrow.

Once the words slipped out, I realized that I shouldn't have said that. It was none of my business what she did. Arthur had hired me for a job, and I wasn't there to judge her on what she did or didn't do. I had no idea what her situation was like.

"Being with Sam seemed exciting at first. He was paying a lot of attention to me. That was something that my husband wasn't doing. But recently I started having regrets. Yesterday, I told Sam I wanted to break things off and try to work it out with my husband." She looked down at her hands. "Now it's too late."

She pulled a tissue from her purse and wiped her eyes. I looked closer to gauge whether they were fake tears, but the truth was, I had no idea. I liked to think I was a good judge of character, but I couldn't read Allison Abbott. I didn't know if she was truly sincere or if this was all an act.

"Why did you come here today?" Determination filled my voice.

"The police think I killed my husband."

I detected a touch of fear in her voice, but then I looked up and noticed her cold eyes. How could she have no emotion? Or how could she hide it? This was getting serious. What did she want me to do about it? Shouldn't she be talking to a lawyer instead of me?

"Are you sure?" I asked.

She wiped her eyes again. "They've been asking a lot of questions."

"Well, I guess they don't have any proof that you murdered him or they would have arrested you by now," I said, proud of my shrewd assessment.

"I don't trust them. They'll find something or make something up. I don't want to go to jail," she said.

I was sure no one wanted to go to jail. Locked behind bars was one of the last places I'd ever want to be. Why was she so sure they would find something against her unless she really was guilty? I found that I wanted out of this situation more and more with each passing minute.

"Do you have an alibi?" I asked, almost afraid of her answer.

Her gaze shifted from mine and she was quiet for a moment. Finally, she answered, "No, I don't have an alibi, per se."

"Well, I guess it's none of my business, but that can't look good to the police," I said.

She released a deep breath, then said, "I was with Sam Louis and then I stopped off at the beach for a walk."

"Did anyone see you at the beach?" I pressed.

She shook her head. "Yes, but the person saw me walking from the beach to the condo tower where my husband was staying."

My eyes widened. "Why in the world were you there?"

My question had come out a teensy bit harsher than I'd intended.

"I wanted to talk to him about our marriage, but I backed out at the last minute and went home," she said.

Oh, she was so screwed. They might as well take her in and snap the mug shot now. I decided to remain positive for her benefit, though. Keep a professional persona, I reminded myself.

"Well, I'm sure they'll find the killer. They always have to talk with the spouse first. You do have an attorney, right?" I looked at her optimistically.

She nodded. "It's the other partner in the firm. His name is Matt Cooper. He's a great attorney and he was good friends with my husband, obviously. I trust him . . . but it's just that I don't trust the police."

Wow, she really had an issue with the police. I wondered what that was about. She stared at me while I formulated in my mind the best way to word my next question.

Finally I asked, "Was Sam Louis involved in the murder of your husband?"

Again, she looked away for a moment before finally turning to look at me again.

"To answer your question, no, I don't think he was." She blew out a deep breath. "Hell, I don't know what to think. Anything is possible, I guess."

I had to admit I was intrigued by this mystery. Who would have killed Arthur Abbott? I'd learned early on in life never to trust anyone. Allison Abbott could be lying to my face. I shouldn't fall for her sweetness or mourning face.

Her eyes were red and puffy. Had she been crying because of her husband or just because she was being accused of his murder?

"How do you know your husband was murdered?" I asked.

It had been fairly obvious to me when I'd discovered the body that he hadn't killed himself, but I had to ask.

She furrowed her brow. "The police told me."

"How exactly did he die?" I asked.

I'd never gotten the specifics from the police. I'd thought it was a gunshot, but I'm no expert.

"He had been shot. The wound wasn't self-inflicted." She wiped her tears again.

Well, there was my answer.

I'd been in the condo. Would she think I'd murdered her husband? Maybe she was coming to me to set me up? This was becoming more of a twisted maze with each second.

I'd have to work my way around the police with this one.

"Excuse me for asking, Ms. Abbott, but why are you here? Why are you telling me all of this?"

"I want you to find the killer," she said matter-of-factly.

My mouth fell open. "I don't know what to say."

"I didn't know where to go for help. You can understand, right?" She looked at me for an answer.

Not really, but that was neither here nor there. "Can't your attorney, Mr. Cooper, help you find the real killer?" I asked.

She paused as she twisted her hands nervously. "Yes, I suppose he could, but he has enough going on right now without

dealing with my problem. I got myself into this mess. I shouldn't have cheated on my husband."

I paused, at a loss for words.

"I can pay you well for your services." She locked her gaze on me.

It was hard to say no when she was looking at me like that. Plus, I needed the money. How the heck had I gotten myself involved in a murder investigation? Wasn't it bad enough that I'd found the body? Now I was supposed to find the killer too? But what did I have to lose? Would it be strange if I took her as a client? What would the police say? What would that Detective Jake Jackson think? Maybe I'd show him a thing or two. He seemed to think that I was incompetent.

I released a deep breath. I was probably going to regret what I was about to do. "Okay. I'll help you, but you have to tell me everything."

She offered a small smile. "Of course. I'll tell you anything you need to know." She pulled out her purse and then her checkbook. "I can write you a check."

I handed her a pen. There was no looking back now.

As Allison Abbott filled out the check, the office door opened and Dorothy marched in. Dressed in bright green pants and shirt, she looked like a giant margarita. She paused for a moment and frowned when she saw Allison sitting in the chair at my desk. She continued to stare as she moved over to her little desk in the corner. Her mouth remained open as she plopped down on the seat.

Allison tore off the check, drawing my attention back to the situation at hand. "Please let me know what other information you need and how much the fee will be. That should get you started, right?"

I looked down at the check and tried to hide my excitement. Yes, it was definitely enough to get me started. But what would I do first? I needed a full rundown of the events of that morning

and the last time she had seen or talked to her husband. I glanced at my watch. Was it too early for lunch? I needed time to devise a plan. Maybe a juicy hamburger would help me think straight. But first I needed to get all the information I could from Allison and to do that I needed to leave the office. With Dorothy staring at us, I couldn't concentrate on the questions I needed to ask.

"Would you like to step outside to the beach? You can answer a few questions and I'll let you get on your way." I motioned toward the door.

She nodded and pushed to her feet. "Sure."

Dorothy frowned at me and mouthed something that I couldn't understand as I followed Allison out the door. I'd deal with Dorothy's twenty questions later.

Allison and I stepped out into the bright sunshine. The seagulls shrieked, still hovering around the area, but there seemed to be fewer of them today. The sun was already hot, bathing my exposed skin in warmth.

We stepped out onto the sand and it squished under my feet. The waves lapped lazily at the shore. We walked for a moment before I spoke.

Finally, I said, "When was the last time you saw your husband?"

"The last time I saw him was the day before he was murdered. He was relentlessly asking me questions. I told him I didn't want to discuss it and I left. When I returned, he'd left a note for me telling me that he'd moved out," she said with a sigh.

"You said he moved to the condo. That was the place where I found him, right?" I asked.

I hadn't thought to ask Allison if she knew that I'd discovered the body, but based on her expression, I figured the police had already told her.

She nodded. "Yes. I never knew why he'd bought the place. He let Matt Cooper talk him into it. Arthur always was easily persuaded."

"Why does that building seem abandoned?" I asked.

"Because it is abandoned." She glanced over at me.

"What do you mean?"

She pushed a strand of hair behind her ear. "Arthur was a stubborn man. He didn't want to leave that building. The developers offered him a condo in the tower next door, but he declined to take it. Everyone else who lived in the building took the offer, but Arthur refused to take the deal. The owner had lost a lot of money on the tower because he couldn't sell all the units. Like I said, Arthur was stubborn like that. The owner of the building wasn't happy with him because of that."

Would the owner of the condo building do something drastic to Arthur? I'd have to find this man and ask questions.

"Why did the owner want the people to leave the tower?" A wave of water splashed against my ankles.

"They had a buyer for the whole tower, but not if Arthur was still living in his condo." She glanced over at me.

"Oh, I guess that makes sense," I said.

"In all fairness, I think Arthur wasn't getting a good deal on the transaction," Allison said.

"Is there anything else you can think of? Is there any person who might have done this to your husband?" I pressed.

She looked straight ahead, lost in thought. After a few seconds, she shook her head and said, "I can't think of anyone. Like I said, the man who owned the building wasn't happy with him. Matt tried to convince Arthur to take the other condo, but he wouldn't do it."

"Do you have the name of the building owner?" I asked.

She waved her hand. "I really didn't keep up with any of his business transactions, so I'm not sure. I believe his first name was Thomas, but I'm not sure."

She really was clueless. "Could you find out for me? I'd like to speak with him."

"Sure, I'll find out and let you know." She motioned over her shoulder. "Well, I'd better get going. I have a lot of things to take care of now."

"I'll call you as soon as I have information for you," I said.

I hoped I hadn't fallen for an act. What if she'd really killed her husband?

Chapter Seven

After leaving Allison, I headed back into my office. Dorothy placed her knitting needles on her desk and glared at me. "What was that all about? Wasn't that the woman who was cheating?"

I ignored her stare and walked to my desk. "Yes, she wants me to help find her husband's killer."

"Oh dear. This is just too strange. I don't trust these people one bit. First the husband comes in and the next thing you know he's deader than a doornail, then his crazy wife comes in here. You'd do well if she lost your address and never came back." She wiggled her finger.

"Dorothy, is that any way to treat a client?" I asked.

"You didn't agree to take the case, did you? Even your crazy Uncle Griffin would have turned her down," she said.

I shrugged. "I have to do what I have to do. Plus, I'm not Uncle Griffin."

Dorothy shook her head and started knitting feverishly, all the while mumbling under her breath.

I had little to go on to solve Arthur's murder, but I'd have to work with what I had. Was the man in the building Arthur's killer? If so, who was he and how would I find him? If the building was empty other than Arthur's condo, then it would be unlikely I'd find anyone else there. Plus, the owner had given me a strange look when I'd mentioned Arthur's name. Well, I assumed the peculiar

man was the owner, but I didn't know for sure. Allison said the owner of the tower wanted Arthur out. Had that man been the owner? It shouldn't be too hard to find out.

I needed to speak with Sam Louis and Matt Cooper. It would be an awkward conversation with Sam Louis, to say the least. Did Matt Cooper know about the affair? I hoped the police didn't get in my way. Specifically Jake Jackson.

An hour had passed and after doing a simple Internet search, I had a home address for Sam Louis. I'd stop by and ask him a few questions and find out if he had an alibi. I grabbed my bag and headed for the door.

"Where are you going?" Dorothy asked.

"I have to ask Sam Louis a few questions to find out if he has an alibi," I said with my hand on the doorknob.

"Do you think he'll be honest with you?"

I shrugged. "I don't know, but there's only one way to find out."

Dorothy grabbed her purse and dumped the knitting needles inside. She rooted around in the bag until finally pulling out a tube of lipstick and little compact mirror.

She smeared the bright red color over her mouth and then, smacking her lips together, looked up at me. "Well, let's go. I have to plan the Bunco party tonight and want to be back in plenty of time to pick up the alcohol."

I stared at her for a moment, then said, "I think this is something I should do on my own."

"Oh, don't hand me that load of crap. Now let's go." She grabbed her bag and marched toward the door.

As I approached my car, the sense of someone following me overwhelmed me, so I whipped around. I would attack the person behind me before they had a chance to attack me. Jake Jackson stood behind me. His eyes widened when he saw my fists in the air in defensive mode. I was trained in self-defense. Well, I'd taken a

couple classes. I'd never actually used any of the techniques I'd learned, but I'd use them today if I had to.

"Whoa. What's going on?" he asked, holding his hands up in surrender.

"Don't walk up on someone like that. It's a good way to get punched." I clutched my chest.

He smiled, but didn't respond.

"What do you want?" I snapped.

Okay, I was on the defensive already and he'd only uttered a few words. Dorothy had ignored Jake and climbed into my car, pulling out her crossword puzzle. She wasn't much help.

"You've been in contact with Allison Abbott?" he asked.

I folded my arms in front of my chest. "Maybe I have. Why do you ask?"

"She's been arrested for the murder of her husband, Arthur Abbott," he said matter-of-factly.

It felt like I'd been punched in the stomach. Jake Jackson had attacked me with his words. What would I do now? How would I continue? Allison was paying me to find the killer, but was I searching in vain?

I shook my head. "She didn't murder him."

It had been the first thing I could think to say. For some strange reason I felt as if I had to defend her.

"What makes you think that?" he asked.

"What makes you think that she murdered him?" I countered.

"I can't give that information to you. This is an active investigation," he said.

Why hadn't Allison's lawyer contacted me? I'd have to call him immediately. I needed to plan my next move though . . . and quickly. This curveball had taken me off guard.

"Allison has hired me to find her husband's killer." I stood a little straighter.

"Well, you can stop your investigation now," he said.

"What? Are you serious?" I snorted. "I intend on finding the killer."

"You need only look in the Dade County Jail to find her." Jake studied my face.

I glared. "You think you're so clever, but I'm not giving up that easily."

He ran his hand through his thick black hair. "Look, I'm not trying to give you a hard time. I'm just trying to help you."

I pointed. "I don't need your help."

His mouth eased into a teasing smile.

"Why are you smiling at me?" I demanded. "This isn't a laughing matter."

"You're pretty when you're angry," he said.

I scoffed. "You can't be serious?"

That was the last thing I wanted to hear right now. Okay, it was kind of nice to hear, but I wouldn't let him know that. It would only encourage this behavior.

"Would you like to grab some lunch and we can discuss this further?" he asked, gesturing over his shoulder.

I quirked a brow. "I have a case to figure out."

"What makes you so sure that she is innocent?" he asked.

I paused, then said, "Because she told me so."

He snorted. "You've got a lot to learn. All the criminals are innocent. Don't you know that?"

"Did you come here just to insult me?"

"What about if I help you out?"

"What does that mean?" I asked.

He stuffed his hands into his pockets. "Well, if she's innocent then I could help you hunt down the real killer."

There had to be a catch. What was this guy up to?

With my hand on the car door, I said, "But you think the killer has already been caught. I have a case to take care of now, if you'll excuse me."

I hopped into my car and backed out. Dorothy set her crossword puzzle book down.

She peered at me over the top of her eyeglasses. "Well, what was that all about? Did he ask you out on a date? You should definitely go."

"I don't need a date," I said, distracted by what had just happened.

When I glanced back, Detective Jackson was still standing there staring at my car. He had that little smile on his face, which just irritated me. Well, it was a little sexy, but that was neither here nor there.

Chapter Eight

I pulled up to the large white stucco home and parked my car at the curb. I wanted to have a fast getaway if need be. With the way things had been going lately, I never knew what might happen. Sprinklers pirouetted on the lawn and the summery scent of freshly mowed grass floated through the air. Large palm trees towered over the front of the house. I walked up the flower-lined pathway to the front door and rang the doorbell.

No one answered, so after a moment, I pushed the doorbell again.

"I'm coming," someone yelled from the other side of the door.

Finally, the door swung open and a woman looked me up and down with a frown spread across her face. She had dishwater-blonde hair and wore black shorts and a pink blouse. Dark circles ringed her big brown eyes.

"I don't want to donate and I don't want to buy anything," she said as she began to close the door.

Why had she even bothered to answer if she was just going to shut the door in my face before finding out what I wanted? That was just rude.

"I'm not here to sell anything and I don't want your money," I rushed my words.

She stopped and let out a deep breath, although she didn't fully open the door again.

"What do you want?" she asked with frustration in her voice.

"I'm here to speak with Sam Louis," I said with a smile.

I'd figured I'd have better luck speaking with him at his home than dealing with the receptionist-from-hell at the law office.

She looked me up and down. "Who are you?"

I had a decision to make. Should I be truthful with her? Based on the attitude she'd displayed up to this point, I figured she wouldn't be pleased when I told her who I truly was. Nonetheless, I had to be honest.

"My name is Maggie Thomas. I'm a private investigator doing some work for the law firm," I said.

Okay, I'd bent the truth a little. It hadn't been a complete lie, though. I had been working for Arthur Abbott before he'd met with an untimely death. Her expression softened. I'd taken a chance, but it looked as if it was going to pay off.

"I'm really sorry," she said opening the door wide. "I've had a bad day."

If this was Sam's wife, then I had an idea why she'd had a bad day. Had he told her about his affair?

"I'm sorry but he's not here," she said around a sigh.

That was not what I'd wanted to hear. She must have noticed the look of disappointment on my face.

"But I can tell you where to find him. He's at the country club. It's the Palms Course. He'll be there for a while. If you need to speak with him right away, I can call him." She gestured over her shoulder.

I smiled. "Thank you, but that won't be necessary."

He had gone golfing right after his business partner was murdered? And his lover was in jail for the crime? Something was rotten about this scenario and I had to find out what his deal was.

"If you're sure," she said.

I could just stop by and speak with him. I needed to have this conversation in person.

I waved my hand. "I can just swing by there. I was headed that way anyway."

She looked at me suspiciously, but I ignored the expression and took off down the driveway for my car.

When I hopped in, Dorothy said, "She looked snobby. What was her problem?"

"Her husband is having an affair. I'd be in a bad mood too." I cranked the ignition.

I pointed my car in the general direction of the Palms Course and punched the address into the GPS. Thirty minutes later, after fighting traffic, I wheeled the car into the parking lot of the Palms Course. I still couldn't get over the fact that Sam was at a golf course. His partner had been murdered. Didn't he care that Allison was in jail? If he claimed to love her as she said, then how could he be so nonchalant about what had happened?

I found a spot at the back and made the trek across the lot with Dorothy in tow. I walked past the valet parking, looking at it longingly. Would they let someone who wasn't a member onto the golf course? Did I really want to interrupt Sam's game? Maybe I'd just find out how much longer he'd be and wait for him. Who would offer that information to me, though?

"I should have worn my golf clothes," Dorothy said.

"Do you play golf?" I asked.

"No, I just like the look." She adjusted the pocketbook on her arm.

I stared for a couple seconds, then nodded. "Whatever floats your boat."

Dorothy eyed me up and down. "We're going to stand out on the golf course. We should have changed before we came all the way here."

"We didn't have time. Besides I don't plan on being here long."

Dorothy and I made our way across the parking lot, weaving around the golf carts and people with their golf bags. We walked into the lobby and looked around.

"So what's your plan now, genius?" Dorothy said.

I glared at her. "It just so happens I do have a plan. Thank you."

She crossed her arms in front of her chest. "Well, let's hear this great plan."

I cleared my throat. "Okay . . . we'll get a golf cart and drive around the course until we find him."

She snorted. "You can't be serious."

I stared at her. "What's wrong with that plan?"

"Oh, nothing. Please go right ahead." She waved her arm through the air.

I marched over to the counter and noticed that Dorothy wasn't behind me. She was still across the room with her arms folded across her chest.

I stomped back over. "What are you doing? Are you coming with me?"

She stared for a bit, then said, "Just let it be known that I think this is a bad idea. We should just wait until we see him come through here."

"What if he just started playing? It could be hours."

She looked at me for a second as if my words were stirring in her head. "I guess you have a point."

"Okay. Good. Now let's get a cart." I motioned for her to follow.

I asked the teenage boy behind the counter where to get a cart and he pointed me in the right direction. After securing the cart, I walked over and found that Dorothy had already positioned herself behind the steering wheel.

"What do you think you're doing?" I asked as I marched over.

"I'm driving the golf cart." She beamed.

I shook my head. "Oh no. Not after the way you drive that Cadillac."

She narrowed her eyes and puckered her lips. Finally she said, "Either I'm driving or I don't go."

I wanted to tell her to stay, but she looked determined.

I let out a deep breath, then said, "Fine, but be careful. And for heaven's sake, don't run over anyone."

With a lurch we took off down the golf path looking for Sam. I soon realized that there were a lot of people playing. How would I find him in the groups of people? Dorothy's driving hadn't been bad after that shaky start, but the longer she drove the faster she went. The driving was made only slightly better by the fact that we were going uphill. But everything that goes up must come down, and I wasn't looking forward to that.

I had no idea a golf cart could even go that fast. I held on to the side, praying that she didn't tip the thing over.

"Dorothy, where's the fire?" I yelled. "We can't even see anyone because you're going too fast."

Up ahead I spotted the downhill descent. I said a silent prayer as the cart sped out of control down the hill. We were almost at the bottom when Dorothy finally slammed on the breaks as she tried to navigate a sharp turn. Unable to hold on any longer, I tumbled out of the cart, landing flat on my face. Luckily, I'd landed on the soft grass instead of the sidewalk. That concrete path would not have been my friend. I pushed my body up with my hands. Nothing seemed to be broken. And, surprisingly, the pain wasn't too bad.

"Maggie, I am so sorry. The speed got a little out of hand," Dorothy said as she shuffled over.

"A little out of hand? You think?" I pushed to my feet with a groan. "I'm driving this time." I stomped over to the driver's side and Dorothy didn't argue.

It had taken me almost being killed before she'd relinquished the steering wheel.

We'd been around practically the whole golf course and I still hadn't spotted Sam Louis. I was beginning to think I was wasting my time. I knew Dorothy thought we were wasting time.

She'd much prefer a crossword puzzle book and a tall glass of tea at the moment. Heck, I'd rather be on the beach reading a book, but work came first.

As we neared the end of the golf path that led back to the clubhouse, I noticed a man watching us. He was walking our way. Uh-oh. Hey, I'd paid for this golf cart and hadn't broken any laws. Other than the little accident, we had been angels the whole time we had been on the course. I mean, what could he possibly think Dorothy was doing wrong? For all he knew she was looking for her grandson.

When the man approached, he said, "I couldn't help but notice that you ladies seem to be looking for someone. Can I help you?"

I looked him up and down. "Do you work here?"

He smiled. "Yes, I do."

After a pause, I said, "Well, I'm looking for a Sam Louis. I'm sure you don't know him. There must be a lot of people who come through here on a daily basis."

"Attorney Sam Louis?" he asked.

I nodded, "Yes, that's him. Was he here today?"

"It's funny you ask about him. He is very popular today."

I frowned. "What do you mean?"

"There was a private investigator here just a short time ago looking for him," he revealed.

I looked at Dorothy. She was clearly as shocked by this revelation as I was.

"Did this private eye give you his name?"

The man furrowed his brow in concentration. "No, I don't remember. Sorry. It was a young man with dark hair. He was probably your age."

"Did he say why he was looking for Sam Louis?" I asked.

He shook his head. "No, but I figured it had something to do with the news of his partner's death. You know about that? Arthur Abbott was a member of this course too. He was a very nice man. He will be missed—"

Dorothy cut him off, “Well, is Sam Louis still here?”

He pointed across the golf course. “I’m not sure, but I think his car was still in the parking lot a few minutes ago.”

“Do you know if this man spoke with Mr. Louis?” I asked.

I’d certainly gotten more news than I’d anticipated from this man.

“Yes, I saw them speaking with each other.”

“But you don’t know what about?” I pressed.

He shook his head. “No, I didn’t listen.”

I waved. “Okay, well, thank you for the help.”

“You’re welcome.” He turned to walk away, then paused and looked at us again. “Oh, one more thing: I did see him get a phone call as he was walking away. He rushed away as he was talking on the phone.”

“Thanks again,” I said.

I wondered who had called him. Would he have rushed away once he’d learned Allison was in jail? After turning in the golf cart, we scanned the parking lot looking for Sam Louis’s car. It wasn’t in the same spot where I thought I’d seen it earlier. He must have left as soon as he’d gotten the phone call. So much for asking him questions. But who was this private investigator? And why was he looking for Sam?

Chapter Nine

The next day arrived and I had another mission. With the leads that I had, I needed to do a little investigating. If only I could sneak into Arthur's condo without the police finding out about it. I surely didn't want that Detective Jake Jackson snooping around.

Even if I couldn't get into Arthur's condo, I'd at least check out the building's perimeter. Allison had said everyone who had lived there moved and now lived in the tower next door. Maybe someone at the other tower had seen or heard something. It was worth a shot to ask around.

Within twenty minutes, I was pulling up to the Towers of Coral. The coral-colored building overlooked the gleaming Atlantic Ocean. Crime scene tape was still draped across the main door leading into the lobby. Little good it was, though, because I could easily slip under it. Arthur's condo door had been busted, so maybe the police hadn't bothered to secure it after they'd finished collecting evidence. The broken door went against my theory of someone Arthur knew having committed the crime. I'd have to figure that part out later.

I parked the car on the street by the curb rather than pulling into the parking lot. The last thing I needed was to draw attention to the fact that I was the only car there. I grabbed my gun this time and secured it in its holster. Glancing to my left and right, I didn't notice anyone around so I made my way across the parking

lot toward the front door of the building. The smell of the salty air wafted around me.

I'd almost made it to the door when I heard movement nearby. It sounded like someone was walking behind me. I whipped around, but saw no one. Suddenly a bullet whizzed by my arm. I jumped into the nearby overgrown bushes and pulled out my gun. My heart hammered in my chest as I waited for the next shot to be fired. An eerie silence fell over the area. Had I imagined being shot at? Maybe it had been a car backfiring. I leaned out a bit, but no other shots rang out. For that, I was thankful. Who in the hell was shooting at me? The air around me was still silent. I looked to my left, right, and even up, not knowing where my assailant had hidden. When I glanced to my left, I noticed a hole in the building's exterior. I knew it hadn't been my imagination. Someone really had shot at me.

"Maggie, are you okay?" A male voice called out.

I peeked over the bush and saw Jake Jackson hiding by the front gate with his gun drawn. He glanced to his left and right.

"I'm okay . . . I think," I said trying to catch my breath. "Someone shot at me!"

"You can put your gun away and come out. Whoever it was ran away. I called for backup and the police are searching the area for him now." The detective moved closer to me.

A voice in my head told me to stay hidden and not to release my tight grip on the gun. But reluctantly, I finally placed it back in its holster and eased out from behind the bushes.

"Come with me." Jake grasped my arm and guided me toward the front gate of the parking lot.

"I didn't need to be saved," I said as we made it back to the sidewalk.

"I never said you did, but someone was shooting at you. That's a serious matter, don't you think?" The lines of worry deepened along his brow.

"How did you know I was there and that someone had shot at me?" I asked, trying to hide the annoyance in my voice. I hated that he'd had to save my ass.

He shoved his gun in his holster and looked around, avoiding my gaze. I wasn't going to let him off the hook, though, so I continued to stare.

Finally, he looked at me and said, "I may have followed you."

I felt my blood pressure spike. "You followed me? Why would you do that?"

He shrugged. "I wanted to see what you were up to."

"I'm trying to find the killer, that's what I'm up to. By the way, do you believe me now that Allison isn't the killer?" I asked.

He stared for a beat, then said, "I understand why you feel this way, but there's compelling evidence against her."

"Yet you can't tell me what this evidence is?" I scowled.

"No, I can't, but I can assure you we'll find out who was shooting." Underneath his stern expression was a hint of a smile, flickering like a sensuous flame.

"Why bother? I'll figure that out myself." I folded my arms in front of my chest.

I decided to ignore the exasperated look he gave me.

"We'll need you to make a statement about what happened. I can drive you to the station," he said.

As we made our way over to his car, the police arrived, swarming the building.

"I'll just be a minute while I talk to them." He gestured over his shoulder.

Jake opened the car door and I hopped into the passenger seat. He probably wanted to cuff me and shove me in the back. A faint smile twisted the corners of his lips as he stared at me. I expected a sarcastic comment about me staying put while he talked to the cops, but he didn't say a word. He closed the door and walked away.

The police wanted to find out what had happened, and I wanted to keep them from hindering my investigation. Despite my reservations, I would reluctantly tell the police what had happened and sign a statement at the police station, but I wouldn't agree to drop this case. Besides, there wasn't much to tell. I had my suspicions about who had been involved in the shooting, though. It had to be the man who had been at the building the day I found Arthur's body. Who else would have been wandering around the place?

I had told the police about the strange man on that day, but I doubted that they'd followed up on that lead. There was no doubt in my mind that the creepy old man had been hiding around there that day; he had been the only other person around the crime scene and they'd totally ignored it. Now someone had fired shots at me when I returned to the building. That couldn't have been a coincidence.

Just when I was about to give up and sneak back to my car, Jake climbed into the driver's seat and cranked the engine.

"So what were you doing back at the building?" He asked as he pulled out onto the road.

I was surprised it had taken him this long to ask that question.

"I think we both know what I was doing there," I said, studying my freshly painted pink fingernails.

He glanced over at me. "I'll pretend I didn't hear that."

I shrugged. "Sounds good to me."

"What did you think you'd find at the crime scene? We already got all the evidence." He kept his eyes focused on the road, not glancing my way, although I had the feeling he was watching me out of the corner of his eye.

"Maybe you did, maybe you didn't. Besides, I wanted to figure out a few things based on the layout of the place." I tapped my fingers nervously against the seat.

"Is that right, Sherlock?" The corner of his mouth twisted into a lopsided grin.

"Yeah, that's right," I mimicked.

"So, Maggie Thomas, what made you become a private investigator?" He flashed me a gorgeous smile, exposing his dimples.

"I was thrown into it" didn't sound like a great reason, so I figured I'd skim over that part.

"It was my uncle's agency, so I decided to take it over when he died. My father was a police officer, but he was killed when I was two. I never knew him." I peered out the window, avoiding his gaze.

My mom hadn't even told me about my father until I decided I wanted to be a cop. I'd never known him, but when I told my mother my plans for my criminal justice degree, she'd finally told me the truth about Dylan Thomas. He'd been killed in the line of duty. After all those years of my believing he'd just taken off and abandoned us, she'd revealed that he had actually been murdered. I still couldn't wrap my mind around why she would lie about something like that. But apparently, after he'd died, she'd totally wanted to block it out. In her mind it was better for me to think he'd left us for another woman than to think he was dead.

After she'd told me what happened, I decided that in order to ease her fears about my safety, I would choose a different career path. I guess I hadn't kept that promise now, considering I had been shot at and found a dead guy.

My mother was on her fifth marriage. The last time we'd spoken a few days ago she had been on her way to Las Vegas with her new husband for their six-month wedding anniversary. Stan was an okay man, I guessed. He wore a little too much cologne and had a serious comb-over, but from what I'd seen, he loved my mother and wanted nothing more than to make her happy. That was the most important thing to me. When I'd decided to take over the agency, my mother had stopped talking to me. She swore she wouldn't speak to me ever again. She'd called twenty minutes later and apologized.

I'd already decided to try to hunt down my father's killer. It had been twenty-six years since his murder, and the crime had yet to be

solved. He'd been ambushed one night on his way home from work. A couple weeks later, my mother had packed our bags and moved us to Florida from Kentucky. I had been two years old at the time, as I said, and didn't remember any of what happened. Apparently my mother had wanted to put distance between us and the tragedy. As if that would somehow make it go away. Once I finally discovered the truth, I'd spent many hours researching the case. So far I had no solid leads, but I wasn't about to give up.

Jake didn't offer a comment about my father in return and I was grateful. There was really nothing else to say. He did, however, offer condolences. "Sorry about your father and uncle," he said after a pause.

"Thank you. So how long have you been with the police?" I asked, trying to be polite.

"I've been with the department about seven years now." His smooth voice filled the car with warmth.

In spite of trying to avoid looking at Jake Jackson, I found myself glancing over when I thought he wasn't watching me. He had a confident air about him, but it wasn't arrogance, just effortless self-assurance. As much as I didn't want to admit it, I was slightly intrigued ... *slightly* being the key word.

"Are you from around here?" he asked.

"No, I just moved here from Pensacola when I took over the business," I said.

We pulled into the police station parking lot and Jake hopped out of the car. He had already walked around to my side when I opened the door. Was he trying to open the car door for me?

The station was full of people. Everyone seemed like they knew exactly what they were doing or why they were there. However, I was sure I looked as clueless as I felt. Jake led me back to his office. It was sparse with a desk in the middle of the room and two metal chairs in front. The top of the desk was covered with papers. A photo sat on the far corner of the desk and I wanted badly to know

who was in it. A wife? A girlfriend? What the hell was wrong with me? Why did I care who was in his photo? When he was busy at his computer, I leaned over and tried to get a better look at the picture.

"That's my mother and sister," he said without looking at me.

Damn it. Did he have to do that?

"They're very pretty," I offered.

"Thank you," he said as he turned to look at me.

Another officer came into the room with us. I was happy he'd entered and stopped the staring contest going on between Jake and me.

"This is Officer Freeman. He's helping with the case." Jake pointed at the dark-haired man.

"Nice to meet you," I said.

Officer Freeman shook my hand. He stood beside Jake's desk, leaning over and smiling at me every chance he got. Wasn't he supposed to keep up the tough cop image? He looked more like a teddy bear.

"So if you can just write down once again what happened, we'll let you get out of here." Jake handed me a piece of paper and a pen.

His touch brushed against me and electricity ran through my fingers. I wrote my story as quickly as possible and handed him the paper.

"Are you sure you didn't leave anything out?" He tapped the paper with his finger.

"Positive," I said.

Once Jake had written "the end" at the bottom of page I'd written my statement on, he placed the paper on top of a stack to his right.

"If that's all you need, I'll be going now." I pushed to my feet and gestured toward the door.

"Yeah, that's all we need…" His stare made me uncomfortable yet exhilarated. "Let me drive you back to your car."

Another officer popped his head into Jake's office. "Detective Jackson, can I see you for a minute? I have a question about the Rowe case."

Jake looked at me. "You'll wait for me here and I'll drive you back?"

I nodded. "Sure."

He flashed his gorgeous smile and walked out of the room. As soon as he walked out of the room, I peeked out his office door. Jake disappeared around the corner. No one was looking my way, so I made a dash for the front door.

Thank goodness the interrogation was over. I hurried out of the building before Jake could notice I was gone and catch up with me. On my way out of the building I called Dorothy and asked her to pick me up. Of course she wanted to know what the heck was going on, but I told her the explanation would have to wait until she got there.

Once outside, I paced in front of the building, trying to stay close to the side and go unnoticed. When I glanced over my shoulder, I noticed Jake hurrying toward me with a scowl splashed across his face. I looked to my side for an escape route, but instead all I found was a sea of police cars.

"Where are you going?" he called out as he approached.

"I got a ride. You were finished asking questions, right?" I looked around nonchalantly.

He ran his hand through his hair. "Yeah, but I was going to give you a ride back to your car."

I waved my hand dismissively. "That won't be necessary. It's too much trouble."

"It's no trouble at all." He stared at me with his sexy eyes.

For a moment, I was speechless. His big blue eyes had sucked me in. I had to shake it off. "Well, I've already called my assistant. She's on her way." I glanced at my watch.

He looked down, then flashed me another seductive look. I had to stay strong and fight off his charm. "I thought maybe you'd like to get dinner tonight."

My body screamed for me to say *yes*, but my head was saying *no way*. For once I was going to listen to what my head was telling me. That was a rare occurrence.

"I would, but I have other plans already. Some other time, maybe," I said.

That wasn't exactly telling him *no* firmly. I'd just left myself open for him to ask again. What was I thinking? Luckily, I spotted Dorothy's car as she pulled into the police station parking lot. I was never so happy to see that little gray head peeking up over the top of that steering wheel.

"There's my ride now." I pointed at her Cadillac.

His eyes widened. "That's your assistant?"

"She's very good. She worked for my uncle for a long time," I said.

He nodded. "Uh-huh. Well, some other time, then?"

I nodded. "Yeah, sure. Some other time."

His gaze lingered longer than it should have and so did mine. My heart rate spiked almost as much as it had when that bullet had grazed my arm. I turned around and headed toward Dorothy's Cadillac.

"Maggie?" Jake called.

I turned around. "Yes?"

"Please be safe. And don't go back to the building," he said.

I nodded, but there was little chance that I would actually do what he told me to do. Being a private investigator meant I had to investigate. If it meant going back to the scene of the crime, then so be it.

I climbed into Dorothy's car without looking at the detective again. If I did, I might change my mind about that dinner invitation.

"What the heck are you doing at the police department?" Dorothy asked with wide eyes as I closed the door. "What did you do?"

"It's a long story," I said around a sigh.

She snorted. "I'm sure it is. I see you've captured the attention of that handsome detective again. I wouldn't kick him out of my bed for eating crackers."

"Dorothy!" I said.

"Are you going out with him?" She smiled sheepishly.

I studied my fingernails. "No, I am not going out with him."

"That's a huge mistake on your part," she said as she steered the wheel.

"Don't you want to know why I was at the police station?" I asked.

I couldn't believe I was volunteering this information, but at least it would change the subject away from the detective. I didn't want to discuss his piercing blue eyes or his dazzling white smile. No way would I talk about his well-formed muscles and the way he filled out his suit.

"Fine. Tell me why you were at the police station," Dorothy said as she steered the car onto a street.

"When I went to the condo tower today someone shot at me," I said while picking invisible lint off my shirt.

She swerved as she glanced over at me. "Oh dear heavens. What happened? Did they catch the person?"

I shook my head. "No, he ran away."

"Well, did you get a look at him?" she asked.

I shook my head. "No, I never saw anyone."

"Do the police plan on trying to find out who did this? Is someone trying to kill you? Someone is following you." She glanced in her rearview mirror.

I patted her hand. "Don't worry, Dorothy. You need to calm down. No one is following us and I hardly think anyone is trying to kill me on purpose."

I spoke the words, but I wasn't convinced that someone hadn't specifically targeted me. Maybe they didn't want me to find Arthur's killer.

"Maybe no one is trying to kill you on purpose, but I do believe someone is following us on purpose," she said as she glanced in the rearview mirror again.

"What?" I looked in the side mirror.

"That black car back there is making every move we do. Now, normally I'm not a paranoid person, but this is beginning to scare me just a bit." Her brow furrowed with worry.

"Dorothy, you must be imagining things," I said, watching as the car hung with our every move. "Take another turn up ahead and see if the car follows us."

I couldn't let Dorothy know, but the car was disconcerting. How would I get us out of this situation? It wasn't Jake's car, but could he have sent someone else to follow us? Was this the person who had shot at me?

Dorothy made the next left and I watched in the mirror as the black car did the same.

"See, I told you they were following us," she said with a little more panic in her voice.

"Okay, we have to remain calm while I figure out what to do," I said.

Before I had a chance to have the first inkling of a plan, Dorothy punched the gas.

"What are you doing?" I held on to the car door.

"I'm going to lose them." Her eyes had a glazed-over look and I was pretty sure it wasn't cataracts causing the problem.

"Dorothy, you're wild. You'll get us killed," I said.

"Someone has to get that scum-sucking bastard off our ass," she snapped.

Chapter Ten

I had to get a good look at who was following us. It had to be the person who had shot at me. So I had been the intended target after all. There was only one reason someone would want me dead and that was either that they thought that I knew who killed Arthur or they wanted to stop me from finding out who had murdered him.

I pulled my gun out of its holster and craned my neck around for a better look.

"What are you doing with that?" Dorothy asked with wide eyes as she glanced down at the gun.

"If someone starts shooting at us I have to be prepared." I held the gun tightly.

"Seventy years may seem old to you, but I plan on living at least until I'm ninety years old. Besides, I do not want to go out with my hair looking like this." She gestured toward her head. "I haven't been to the beauty parlor in two weeks."

I glanced over at her hair. It looked the same as the other few times I'd seen her. "We're not going to die. I won't let that happen."

"I'm holding you to that. If I get killed and you don't, I'm definitely coming back to haunt you," she warned with a wave of her hand.

"We're going to have to lose this car," I said.

In spite of Dorothy's best efforts, the car was still hanging on to our every move.

"If I can't drive fast, how do you suggest I do something like that?" she asked.

That was a good question. My answer would be nothing but a guess. Sweat had broken out on my forehead and my stomach turned. I had to get this right or Dorothy's fears just might come true.

"Can you weave in between those two cars?" I pointed up ahead.

She wiped her forehead with one hand while steering with the other. The car's air conditioner was cranked to full capacity, but only lukewarm air spilled out from the vents. Of all times for the air to stop working.

"Well, I haven't done any stunt driving for a few years but I can give it a try." She clutched the steering wheel tightly.

I glanced over at her, but honestly couldn't tell if she was joking. Somehow I wouldn't be surprised if she'd actually been a stunt driver.

"You should give it a try, then," I said, trying to sound in control.

"What do I do?" she asked.

I gestured. "Up ahead is an on-ramp for the expressway. You'll have to slip between the cars and then turn off at the last minute. The car behind us won't be able to keep up."

"But what if they do stay with us?"

"That's the chance we'll have to take. I'll think of something else if that happens, okay?" I asked.

She nodded, remaining silent. I was shocked that she hadn't come back with some witty retort.

Dorothy punched the gas again and merged into the left lane. I glanced in the rearview mirror to check on the mystery car. It sped up in an attempt to catch up to us. Dorothy's hands were clutching the steering wheel so hard that I knew it would take pliers to remove them. She whizzed the car into the middle lane between

the two cars. Horns honked all around us. I didn't bother looking over at the pissed-off drivers. I knew I'd get nasty looks and gestures; no need to acknowledge them.

"Okay, turn now!" I yelled.

Dorothy yanked the steering wheel toward the ramp and almost cut off a white van as she zoomed onto the expressway ramp. Horns continued a relentless barrage of warnings.

I looked in the rearview mirror and didn't see the car. When I glanced up at the highway, I saw it driving past. It had tried to slow down, but there was no use. Too many cars were tailgating it.

I released my pent-up breath. "Good job, Dorothy. I didn't know you had it in you."

"You told me to lose the car, didn't you?" she asked.

I smiled. "Yeah, I did tell you that."

I should have known that I wouldn't get away with that car-chasing incident without Dorothy asking for a payback, however. That payback came in the form of a Bunco game.

Chapter Eleven

Dorothy had taken me to her friend Mary's place for Bunco night. Mary lived in a condo complex a couple of blocks from the beach. I'd insisted on driving this time. The living room was full of women. All of them had the same short gray hairstyle. They wore pink baseball caps with BFF written across the front. That stood for Bunco Friends Forever, by the way.

"We'll have to get you a cap," Dorothy said excitedly.

"Yay, I can't wait," I said with false enthusiasm.

This was my punishment for what I'd put Dorothy through. I had tried to buy my way out of it, but I remembered that I really didn't have any money, so that hadn't worked out. Now I was sitting in a sea of women wearing pink baseball caps and dice earrings. The room was even decorated with dice and more dice. I spotted wineglasses with dice painted on each one. At least there was wine.

As Dorothy tried to explain the rules of the game, I found my mind wandering. Thoughts of car chases, bullets, and hot detectives whirled in my head. I hoped whoever had it out for me hadn't followed me here. I sure didn't want to put these women in jeopardy. Until I figured out who was responsible, I had to be on guard everywhere I went.

Dorothy clasped her hands together. "I hope I win the door prize tonight. Mary always has the cutest prizes."

I bit back a chuckle. "I hope you win too, Dorothy. If I win I'll give you the prize, okay?"

"Well, you should after what you put me through. But I doubt you'll win. You have no idea what you're doing." She grabbed the dice.

"The game doesn't seem too complicated. Maybe I can win," I said.

Dorothy snorted and shook her head as if I'd said the most outrageous thing she'd ever heard.

I was just getting the hang of things when the room fell silent. Everyone was staring at the door and I whipped around to see what all the fuss was about. *Please don't let someone with a gun be at the door.* Much to my chagrin, someone with a gun was at the door. Luckily, it wasn't the bad guy.

"Who's the hunk?" one of the women whispered to Dorothy.

What was Jake doing here? How had he found me? Again!

He spotted me right away and smiled. Of course all the women immediately looked at me.

"It must be her boyfriend," a woman whispered. Of course their whispering wasn't really whispering because I was hearing everything they said loud and clear.

"He's not my boyfriend," I said to no one in particular.

"What a beefcake," another woman said around a sigh.

I hurried over to the door so that I could get rid of him before they asked him to stay.

"Why are you here?" I asked.

Jake smiled. "Imagine seeing you here."

"Have you been following me again? This has got to stop. I'm going to be forced to report you to your supervisor if you don't stop stalking me." I folded my arms in front of my chest and glared at him. Sadly, he probably wasn't intimidated by my stern look. I gave it a try anyway.

"Are you finished yelling at me yet?" he asked with a smirk.

I tucked my hair behind my ear. "No. I mean, I'm not sure. Are you going to leave me alone?"

"I can't guarantee that." The side of his mouth twisted into a grin.

"What do you want? I have to get back to my game." I motioned over my shoulder.

"Kiss him, honey," one of the women said from over my shoulder.

The rest of the room broke out in laughter like a gang of thirteen-year-old girls.

He smiled. Finally he said, "You're parked in my spot." He motioned over his shoulder.

I looked out at my car parked in the lot. "What are you talking about?"

He pointed. "I live next door and you've got my reserved parking space."

What were the odds of that? Out of all the places in Miami, he lived next door to my Bunco game.

"I didn't know there was assigned parking." I grabbed my purse and headed out the door.

He followed behind me. "Having a girls' night out?" His voice held a mocking tone.

"If you must know, yes," I said.

"Wow, you are a wild one. I knew it. I could tell by the look in your eyes." He winked.

"You have any new leads on the Abbott case?" I asked, ignoring his comment.

"Like I told you before, I'm not looking for any new leads."

"Well, you should." I stared for a minute, then climbed into my car.

He folded his arms in front of his chest as a wide smile spread across his face. I'd hoped he would go into his apartment after I moved my car, but he waited for me on the sidewalk.

"I moved my car. Don't you want to park yours before someone else steals your spot?" I pointed.

"I doubt anyone else will take the spot," he said.

"Well, I'd better get back to my game. They'll be waiting for me." I motioned over my shoulder.

At least now Jake didn't think that I'd lied to him about being busy tonight. Of course now he knew that I hadn't had a hot dinner date. I wanted to mention the car that had followed us, but I also wanted to get away from his smiling face as soon as possible. After my mental debate, asking him about the mysterious car won out, although I had a feeling even before I asked that it hadn't been Jake who had followed us.

"Are you going to follow me again like earlier today?" I asked.

He frowned. "I didn't follow you today."

Then who the hell had followed us?

I frowned. "Oh, well, I guess I just thought I saw your car."

He looked at me suspiciously, but before he had a chance to ask more questions, I turned around and walked toward the condo.

"I'll see you later, Thomas," he called out.

I glanced back, but quickly turned around again so that he couldn't see my smile.

"Later, Jackson," I retorted.

Chapter Twelve

Later that night after the Bunco game, my sleuthing wasn't over. I'd taken Dorothy to her condo for a change of clothing. Why she insisted on putting on her stakeout clothing, I had no idea. I was afraid to find out what her idea of private investigator clothing consisted of.

After not being able to talk with Sam Louis at the golf course, I felt I needed to go by his home again. His behavior needed closer attention. I decided to do a stakeout and see just exactly what he was up to. If he was connected to the killing in any way, maybe I'd find out.

Dorothy came out of her condo wearing all black like a cat burglar. She was really getting into this stakeout stuff.

"It's not really necessary to wear all black. We're not stealing precious jewels or anything," I said as she climbed into the car.

"I want to blend in with the night. I don't trust you not to get me into some crazy situation." She buckled her seat belt.

"Dorothy, I'm not trying to get you into anything. After all, you did volunteer to come with me," I pointed out.

It was more like she'd insisted, but I left that part out to be nice.

"Well, someone has to watch over you." She frowned.

After ten minutes, we reached Sam's house. The neighborhood was quiet and there were no other cars on the street. I had no idea if we'd catch Sam doing anything, but it was worth a shot.

We pulled up to his house and parked out front. I stayed back so that he wouldn't see my car, although his neighbors would probably notice. As long as they didn't call the police I'd be fine. The last thing I needed was for Jake Jackson to find out what I was doing. We waited for only about five minutes before something odd started happening inside the house.

Lights began going on and off around the house. It was as if someone was going from room to room and turning the lights on, then off rather quickly. It was as if the person was checking each room for someone or something. This happened in every visible window.

"What do you think is going on, Dorothy?" I asked.

"I'd say he is looking for something. Maybe he lost his cat," she said.

That was a possibility, but maybe he was looking for someone. Within a couple minutes, the light show stopped. Then the garage door opened and the silhouette of a man appeared. He moved around in the garage for a few seconds, then finally got into his car and backed out.

We hunkered down in the seat as he pulled out. Maybe Dorothy's idea of wearing all black wasn't that bad an idea after all. At least I would have been less visible if I'd dressed in the same getup.

After a second, I peeked up and saw that the person I'd assumed was Sam was headed down the street. I cranked the engine and began to follow, keeping a safe distance. Where was he headed and what had he been looking for?

"Did you bring your equipment with you?" Dorothy asked.

"Yeah, it's in the case in the backseat." I gestured.

I doubted anything in that silver case was going to help me tonight, though. Would I be able to get close enough to eavesdrop? He could be going out for a late-night snack for all I knew.

I'd stayed back a few car lengths as we moved down the highway. He turned a few times and I made sure to try to stay back, but not lose him at the same time. It wasn't as easy as it looked when they did it in the movies. Just as I'd made a right onto the next street, he sped up. I had to punch the gas in order to keep up. Sam was onto me, but did he know that it was me? Regardless, he knew that someone was following him. I'd blown my cover and this was not good.

It seemed as if he was just driving in circles. He turned left, and then right, then left again. Once I turned down Water Street, he was nowhere in sight.

I pounded the steering wheel. "Damn it. We lost him."

"You gave it your best shot, dear," Dorothy said in a sweet voice.

Releasing a sigh, I stepped on the gas and drove a couple of blocks. I turned onto Main Street again and had traveled a few more blocks when his car came into view again. It was a miracle. I may not have been able to keep up, but I had him now and I didn't intend to let him out of my sight this time.

He wasn't driving as fast this time. Could it be possible that he hadn't noticed me following him again? There was more traffic on the main street, but I figured he'd look into his rearview mirror again soon and spot me. After a few more blocks, I followed his car to the public beach entrance. I parked my car across the street and cut the lights. He pulled into the parking lot, stopping his car near a small bench by the entrance to the beach. So far he hadn't looked in our direction. If only I could keep it that way.

After a minute, Sam stepped out of his car and walked toward the beach. He stood there with his back to us for at least a minute. He never turned around as he looked out at the water. Maybe he'd just wanted to watch the ocean and I'd followed him like some kind of crazy woman. I was surprised that he hadn't

called the police to report me. Another minute went by and then he turned around. I hunkered down in the seat, but continued to watch him. He looked to his left and right, then sat on the bench next to him.

As he waited on the park bench, he continued to survey his surroundings. Luckily, the area where I'd parked was dark and at an angle that I didn't think he could see. Although if there was one thing I remembered learning from Uncle Griffin, it was this: If you can see them, they can see you. It made sense.

What did I have to lose, though? If Sam saw me, I'd just take off. If not, then I could continue to snoop on him. Dorothy pulled out a peppermint candy and pushed it toward me. She had a knack of pulling those things out at the most inopportune times.

Dorothy shifted in her seat and I knew she was getting restless. Just when I was ready to give up and go home, a black SUV pulled up and parked right beside Sam's car. The driver cut the headlights right away. A tall man stepped out of the vehicle and walked over to Sam. So he had been meeting someone here after all. My instincts had been right.

Without wasting any time, I pulled out my camera and snapped a few photos. Maybe I'd be able to identify the person he was talking to. It was dark, though, and odds were not in my favor. All I could do was watch from a distance and try to read their body language.

"Sam doesn't know me. I could walk by and try to hear what they're saying," Dorothy offered.

"That's sweet, Dorothy, but I don't want to put you in any danger. It's just not worth it," I said.

She shrugged. "You know I'm not afraid."

"I know, and that is probably not a good thing," I pointed out.

We watched in silence as the men had a conversation. I'd rolled the window down, hoping to pick up bits and pieces of their conversation, but the sound of the surf made it impossible to hear

what they'd said. They seemed to remain calm. Their talk didn't seem heated and neither appeared on the verge of punching the other one. The tall guy handed Sam something. It looked like a file folder, but I couldn't be sure.

After a few moments, the men stopped talking and got back into their vehicles. They cranked their engines and pulled out onto the street. Dorothy and I hunkered down again. It was probably useless trying to follow them, but I'd come this far: I had to at least give it a shot.

Just as I peeked up from my hunkered-down position, Sam's car had turned around and was headed down the street opposite of the way he'd turned out of the lot. That was good for me, though, because my car was already pointed in his direction. I sat up straight and pulled the car out onto the road. I followed Sam down the highway again, but this time the car that had pulled up to talk with him was behind me. He hadn't been there a moment ago. Headlights glimmered, reflecting off my rearview mirror.

Panic ran through me. Was this car following me now or was it just a coincidence? That question was answered soon enough when I glanced in the rearview mirror and saw the SUV riding my bumper. They were trying to intimidate me. And to be honest, it was working a little bit. I had to remain calm. It was time for me to get out of this situation. I'd turn down the next street and let the two of them drive off into the night.

When I took the next right, the SUV followed me. So now the chaser was the chased. This wasn't how I'd envisioned this scene turning out.

"That car is following us," Dorothy said as she turned around.

"Don't look at them," I said.

I stomped on the gas, but the speed limit was twenty-five and I couldn't drive much faster since there were other cars on the road. The SUV didn't seem to mind if it caused an accident, though. As a matter of fact, I think they wanted me to have an accident.

After a couple more turns, I was able to pull into a parking lot. I managed to hide out and waited for the car to pass. The person behind the wheel must be new at this following cars stuff. Heck, I was an old pro at this point. He hadn't even looked over toward the parking lot. That was like Car Chase 101. I had him right where I wanted him now.

"What are you doing?" Dorothy whispered.

"Why are you whispering?" I asked.

She grinned. "Old habit, I guess."

When I felt that it was safe, I pulled the car out onto the street.

"I'm going to follow this jackass, that's what I'm doing," I said with determination in my voice.

Now I was behind the guy. The chaser became the chased. He wasn't speeding or driving erratically, so that led me to believe that he had no idea I was behind him now. He was probably scratching his head, wondering how I'd gotten away.

He made a left onto Main Street. I eased through the green light and was able to follow him. As far as I could tell, he was headed toward the water. Was he going back to the beach or over to the boat docks? My adrenaline spiked as I navigated the streets behind him.

"Don't forget to write down his license plate number," I told Dorothy. "Just in case we have to report him."

"Report him for what?" Dorothy asked in a panicked tone.

I didn't bother to answer because I wasn't entirely sure.

"How long are you going to follow him?" Dorothy asked.

"Until he leads me somewhere we want to go," I said.

"I don't think he'll take us anywhere we'd want to go."

"You know what I mean," I said with a wave of my hand. "Maybe he'll take us to who's behind the murders."

"Yeah, and maybe pigs will fly someday," she said.

I scowled at her but didn't offer a comeback. When he turned left onto the next street, I knew that he was headed to

the boat docks. If he jumped onto a boat and took off, I'd be out of luck.

The SUV pulled up to the boat docks and I hung back waiting to see his next move. He circled around a couple times and I figured he was looking for someone or something. But finally he pulled his vehicle into a spot and cut the engine.

"Maybe he's waiting for someone," Dorothy offered.

"Yeah, maybe he's waiting for the killer," I said.

Her eyes widened, but she didn't respond. No words were necessary. I pulled out my binoculars to take a look, but all I could see was the back of his head.

After a couple more minutes, his car door opened and I held my breath. Would he look back and spot my car? I'd parked behind another car and hoped that it would offer enough cover for us. We watched as the man climbed out from behind the wheel. He glanced around, but never looked in our direction. He stretched his arms above his head and yawned, then headed toward the docks.

"Where is he going now?" Dorothy asked.

I shrugged. "I guess to the boats. Maybe he owns one of them."

"We may never know." Dorothy frowned.

"That's not likely," I said opening my car door. "I'm going to follow him."

Dorothy grabbed my arm as I started to get out of the car. "No, Maggie, I don't want you to do that."

"It's my job," I said with a cluck of my tongue.

"It's dark out there and you don't know who this man is." She looked around in a panic.

"I can protect myself." I tried to reassure her. "Now, lock the car doors and I'll be back in a couple minutes. Call my phone if anything suspicious happens. Definitely call me if anyone else drives up."

She reluctantly nodded. "Just be careful."

I slipped across the parking lot, praying that the night sky offered me some cover. I had no idea what I was walking into. As I approached the docks, I looked over my shoulder. Dorothy was watching me. She gave a little wave, and for a second, I thought about turning back. But I knew I had to push forward. A collection of masts lined the dock, their pennants fluttering in the wind.

I headed down the pier, watching the boats bob up and down in the water. Soft waves shifted along the top of the water. I knew I'd seen him come this way, so he had to be in one of these boats. Only one boat had lights on, so I assumed that was the one I wanted.

I inched my way over, hoping that he wasn't hiding, ready to attack me. When I reached the boat that was lit up, I walked around the vessel, trying to peek in. Finally, I spotted the man. He was sitting below deck across from another man. I got a good look at his face. He was probably in his mid-thirties with dark hair and five o'clock shadow. I couldn't get a good look at the other man. All I saw were his legs. They both wore jeans and sneakers.

Would they see me peeking in? Since they had the lights on, I assumed they couldn't see me. My mother had always warned me about shutting my blinds so that people couldn't watch me at night. I was glad these guys weren't so concerned about that. What were they talking about? Were they discussing me? Was one of them the killer? Was I next on the killer's list? If so, then I was making it easy for them to find me. I'd never seen the guy who'd followed me before.

My pursuer was a big guy with muscles. Since I couldn't hear their conversation, there was no point in hanging around. I'd have to find out more information about this boat.

Just as I turned around to leave, I spotted a card on the deck by the boat's door. I reached down to get it, but slipped forward. I landed on my knees, catching myself with the palms of my hands. My tumble didn't stop me from grabbing that card, though. I stood up quickly and glanced back at the boat. The men had jumped up.

I knew they'd heard the loud thud of me hitting the deck, although it had probably been a faint noise inside the boat. Nonetheless, they were definitely coming to check it out and I didn't want to be anywhere around when they rushed out of that boat. I ran faster than I'd ever run before.

I practically fell onto the car when I reached it. Dorothy looked on in fear. She was looking behind me, so I figured that she'd spotted the men. There was no time for me to look back. I had no idea how close they were. For all I knew they were ready to grab me from behind at any moment. Without wasting another second, I yanked on the car door and jumped in. As I cranked the engine, I glanced up. Thank goodness the men were still standing up by the docks looking around, clueless. They hadn't spotted me, and for that I was thankful. I whipped the car into reverse, then shoved it into drive and took off. If they spotted me pulling off, I didn't even want to know. I didn't look back. I just wanted to get the heck out of there. I still had the card that I'd found.

I shoved it toward Dorothy. "What does this say?"

"There are two addresses. One only has the street, though; no number," Dorothy said.

When I looked in the rearview mirror, police lights were flashing. Oh crap. What had I done? Other than sneaking around a boat dock and spying on a few men? That wasn't illegal, was it? For all they knew I could have been admiring their boat. I pulled the car over to the side of the road.

"Oh, this is just great. We're going to jail and they'll throw away the key," Dorothy said in despair.

"Just try to stay calm and let me do the talking."

When I glanced in my car's side mirror, I spotted Jake Jackson approaching. Damn. This guy just wouldn't leave me alone.

Chapter Thirteen

Sunlight from the one tiny apartment window splashed across my face as an annoying noise chirped in the background. I managed to force my eyelids open and looked around. After a couple more loud rings, I woke up enough to realize my phone was responsible for disturbing my sleep. I shielded my eyes from the bright sunshine and grabbed the phone with my other hand. I didn't bother to glance at the screen to see who was calling. It didn't matter. Whoever it was had better have a good excuse for waking me this early.

"Maggie Thomas," I answered in a groggy, less-than-professional voice.

"Where are you? I've been worried sick," the soft female voice said.

"Mom, is that you?" I asked.

"It's Dorothy and you're late for work," she barked.

I blinked away the blurriness and looked at the clock. It was after nine. How the heck had I slept so late?

"I'm on my way," I said.

Memories of the night before came floating back. After Jake had finally allowed me to leave, I'd eaten cookie dough ice cream right out of the cartoon while I'd spent the late evening hours researching the Abbott case, then moving on to my father's

unsolved murder case. Unfortunately, I'd learned nothing new about either one. Jake had gone back to the boat docks, but apparently the men had already taken off. I wasn't sure if Jake had actually believed me.

I stumbled out of bed and after showering, slipped into blue shorts and a white tank. My professional attire had lasted only a few days. Since I was my own boss, I was officially declaring every day casual Friday.

On my way to the office, I stopped by the little bakery around the corner. They had the best doughnuts. They practically melted in your mouth. As much as I wanted one of the chocolate-glazed ones, I opted for a bran muffin instead. It was no fun, but my waist would thank me later. I decided I needed a little energy pick-me-up after all that I'd been through. The huge sign hung above the door with reminders of the delicious doughnuts. I locked my car and made my way across the parking lot.

The feeling of being watched came over me. When I glanced over my shoulder, I noticed an SUV that looked a lot like the one from last night. It couldn't be the same vehicle again, could it? Who was I kidding? Of course it could be the same one. They probably had my address and followed me here this morning. I needed to be more aware of my surroundings. I was letting my guard down and it was going to get me into deep trouble. I hurried into the shop. I'd see if this person followed me inside. I walked up to the counter and placed my order, then handed my cash to the woman behind the register.

"Do you come here often?" the male voice asked.

I whirled around, ready to defend myself. A little scream slipped from my lips, which after the fact was very embarrassing. I was supposed to be a professional. That was far from professional behavior. I clutched my chest, trying to calm down from the scare.

"I can't believe it's you again," I said with an exasperated tone.

Jake flashed his sexy smile. He looked great even early in the morning, with his rugged good looks and wearing jeans and a faded blue T-shirt.

"What are you doing here?" I asked, blowing my bangs out of my eyes.

He looked over my shoulder toward the baked goods and pointed. "A glazed doughnut."

I stared at him for a moment. He thought he was so clever.

"Why are you following me?" I demanded.

"I can't help it if we live close to each other." He flashed his gorgeous smile.

Yeah, that was what he claimed, but still, it was a big city and I wasn't buying his excuse that it was just a coincidence. The woman handed me the bag with my cardboard-flavored muffin and skinny cinnamon dolce latte. When Jake began placing his order, I started to walk away. I'd barely moved when Jake grabbed my arm. I glared up at him.

"Please don't go," he said with a pleading look.

I released a deep breath. Jake had a way of knocking the air out of me with just a look.

I nodded. "Fine."

After waiting for Jake to get his order, I headed toward the door and he walked along beside me. We reached the door and he held it open for me.

When we stepped outside into the warm morning air, he asked, "Did you get any sleep last night?"

"Why do you ask?" I looked at him suspiciously.

"After your exciting evening I just wondered if you were able to sleep." He looked me up and down and I suddenly became very aware of his intoxicating gaze.

I sipped my drink, then said, "I guess I got enough sleep."

He smiled softly. "Good."

I peeked over at him. "What about you?"

He shook his head. "No, I didn't sleep much. I had a lot on my mind."

I looked over at him again. He didn't offer a reason for his lack of sleep and I didn't press for an answer. My heart sped up.

Jake walked me to my car and we paused by my door.

"Well, I guess I'd better get to work." I tucked a strand of hair that had escaped from my hastily pulled-up ponytail behind my ear.

"You have a full day ahead of you?" Jake casually leaned against my car.

I took another drink. "Yes, I have a murder case to solve."

He shook his head.

"What?" I quirked my eyebrow questioningly.

"Oh, nothing." His mouth curved into a smile. "You're certainly very determined."

I pasted a smile of nonchalance on my face. "I guess I've always been that way."

"It's a good quality." A smile remained on his handsome face.

I knew by the look on his face that he was sincere.

After a pause, I said, "Well, enjoy your doughnut."

Just then a car engine revved and caught our attention. I'd forgotten about the mysterious SUV.

I caught a glimpse of the driver's face as the vehicle peeled out of the parking lot and it was the same man from last night. My stomach turned and panic set in. Who was this man and why was he following me? He'd followed me after I'd followed him, but what did he want? What did Sam know about this? I intended to ask him that question as soon as I tracked him down.

"That was the car from last night," I said in a panic. "Do you believe me now? Do you believe me when I say someone is following me?"

He scowled. "Hop in and we'll see if we can catch up with him," he said as he hurried toward his car.

I ran over to the other side and jumped in, slamming the door behind me. Jake turned the ignition and shoved the car into drive, peeling out of the parking space and flying across the parking lot. A couple people on the other side of the lot stared at us in shock. Jake flipped on his siren and lights, which made my adrenaline flow even more. At that moment a flash of my father's face ran through my mind. Was this a hint of the adrenaline he'd felt on the night of his murder?

We pulled out onto the street, weaving in and out of traffic as cars cleared a path for us. We whizzed past the buildings and cars like they were standing still.

"I don't think we're going to find him." I held on tightly.

"We won't give up just yet. Unless he turned off, he'll be sitting in the traffic up here. It always gets congested," Jake said.

The car came into view.

"That's it right there," I said as I pointed toward the SUV.

Jake sped up and weaved around a couple cars. Within a few seconds, we'd reached the SUV. Finally, I'd find out who this person was and why he was following me. Jake sounded his siren again and the car pulled over to the side of the road. Jake called in the license plate number, then climbed out of the car. I held my breath as I waited for what might happen. This could turn serious at any moment. Jake walked around to the driver's side of the SUV. The driver was a woman. Who the heck was that? He talked to her for a moment, then she pulled the SUV away from the curb.

I didn't want to even look at Jake when he returned to the car.

"That wasn't the guy from last night, huh?" I said feeling more than a little embarrassed.

"Unless he was a girl, then no," Jake said.

"You just followed the wrong car. I know that was the guy from last night in the parking lot. I looked right at his face."

Jake stared in silence for a moment, then said, "I believe you. I can follow you to your office."

I shook my head. "No, that isn't necessary. I'll be fine," I said.

I wasn't so sure about that, but I didn't want Jake to know.

Jake dropped me off at my car and I hurried to the office, ready to put this morning's embarrassing incident behind me.

Chapter Fourteen

When I arrived at the office, Dorothy had left a note stating that she'd be back in an hour. Apparently there had been a surprise sale on yarn and she didn't want to miss the bargains. That was fine with me. I'd spend more time researching.

I was lost in my Internet searching when Dorothy came back with a bag full of yarn.

She placed her hands on her hips and looked at me over the top of her eyeglasses. "Well, I'm glad you made it and I didn't have to send out a search party. I guess last night was just too much partying for you."

The sad truth was it had been exhausting. With the Bunco and the car chase, I had been drained. I really needed to get out more.

I'd spent the last hour working on clues for all my suspects, which consisted of a short list: the condo owner, Sam Louis, and my client. There had to be someone else who hated Arthur Abbott enough to kill him, right? I just didn't want to think his wife or partner would have anything to do with his murder. The condo tower owner, on the other hand…

Dorothy had just sat down when I jumped up.

"Where are you going?" Dorothy asked as I grabbed my purse and headed toward the door.

"I have to do something. This case is going nowhere and now someone is after me," I said.

"Why don't you just tell the police? After all, they know someone tried to shoot at you, and then the car chase. Plus, Detective Jackson seems more than willing to help you out," Dorothy said.

I shook my head. "No way. I'm doing this on my own. A private eye doesn't go running to the police the first time something goes wrong."

"So what are you going to do?" she asked.

"I'm headed to talk with the other partner in the law firm. I also want to talk with the receptionist. She had to know the comings and goings of everyone at the firm. It will probably lead nowhere, but it's better than sitting around doing nothing."

As I reached out to grab the doorknob, Dorothy jumped up and grabbed her purse. "I'm coming with you. You can't talk to that bulldog on your own."

Dorothy had given the receptionist a nickname after I'd told her about her stubborn demeanor.

"What? No way, Dorothy." I shook my head. "Besides, who will answer the phone?"

She smirked. "You can forward the hundreds of calls to your cell phone like you did before. But don't ask me to do it because I don't even know how to check my voicemail."

It looked as if I'd lost that argument. Within a few minutes, Dorothy and I pulled up in front of the office building.

When I shoved the car into park, Dorothy stuffed her knitting needles into her purse and opened the door. "I'm going with you."

Dorothy was being awfully protective now. My own mother had never been that protective. There was no sense in arguing with her.

I made sure to keep my eye out for any suspicious behavior as we made our way across the parking lot. As soon as I stepped into the building, the receptionist looked up at me and frowned. What did this woman have against me? She hadn't liked me from day one.

"May I help you?" She eyed me suspiciously.

"I'd like to see Mr. Cooper," I said, looking her right in the eyes.

I wouldn't let her intimidate me. After all, I could be a client for all she knew.

"Do you have an appointment?" she asked with a frown.

"No, I don't, but it's very important that I speak with him," I said.

She shook her head. "I'm sorry, but he doesn't see anyone without an appointment."

Dorothy marched up to the counter and placed her hands on her hips. "Now listen here. This is an official investigation and we have questions that need to be answered, so I suggest that you go get him right now."

The receptionist stared at Dorothy with her mouth open.

Dorothy continued her rant. "Listen here, lady, you'd better quit messing around with us and just give us the freakin' information."

I had no idea Dorothy's voice could even reach that level.

"You can't talk to me that way," the woman said.

Dorothy tapped on the woman's desk. "Now, do I have to get the information from you the hard way?"

"Dorothy, please." I motioned for her to knock it off. "I'm terribly sorry. My assistant gets a little excited. She had a stroke," I whispered.

"I heard that and I most certainly did not have a stroke," Dorothy said.

I looked at the woman again. She glared at me. Dorothy had certainly riled the hornet's nest, but it looked as if it had been necessary. This woman wasn't about to release any information.

I tapped my fingers against the counter. "Are you going to stop playing games with us and tell me what I need or what?"

"Or what," the woman said in a curt tone.

All right then. That answered my question.

"That's it. I'm coming around that desk." Dorothy moved toward the woman.

"Dorothy, no!"

The woman's eyes widened as I grabbed Dorothy and stopped her from moving around the desk. The receptionist scrambled up from her chair and hurried down the hallway.

"Maybe you could tone it down a notch, Dorothy? I think you scared the woman," I said.

"What? She was like a statue. Nothing would get through to her. I bet the devil is scared of that woman," Dorothy huffed.

"She wasn't that bad," I whispered.

"I think I saw her eyes glow red," Dorothy said.

I chuckled. "Well, just let me handle it next time."

Would there be a next time? I needed to keep Dorothy away from questioning anyone from this moment forward.

"Is there a problem?" a male voice said from over my shoulder.

I whipped around. "Mr. Cooper, you're just the man I wanted to see. If you have a moment, I'd like to ask you a few questions."

He looked just like his photo on the law firm's website. Why hadn't he requested to see me to begin with? He knew that his client had hired me. We should be working together to get her out of jail.

"Please come into my office." He gestured down the hall.

I glanced over my shoulder and caught Dorothy as she smirked at the receptionist. The woman frowned back at Dorothy, matching her dirty look. If I wasn't careful they'd break out into a fight.

Matt Cooper pointed at the chairs. "Please have a seat, ladies. What can I do for you?" he asked.

Dorothy looked around the room, scrutinizing every detail. It was a rather boring space with lots of wood trim and a large walnut desk in the middle of the room. He had a big leather chair behind his desk that resembled a throne. In front of the desk were two small leather chairs. Diplomas and pictures of himself with various fish hung on the walls. On his desk was a picture of a

woman and small children who I assumed were his family. He was much older than she was. He looked old enough to be her father.

"As you know, Mr. Cooper, I'm working for Mrs. Abbott. I just need to ask a few questions," I folded my hands in my lap.

"I understand that Allison has hired you, but really, your services aren't needed."

I stared. "Is that right? And why is that? Do you have someone else investigating the case?"

"That's not something I can divulge," he said curtly.

His answer said it all. Why wouldn't he want to help his client in any way possible?

"Can I just ask some questions about Mr. Abbott?" I asked.

Dorothy sat with her arms in front of her chest, clutching her pocketbook. Her laser-like death glare was focused on Mr. Cooper. It didn't go unnoticed by him, either. He kept glancing at her every few seconds.

"What would you like to know?" He asked as he leaned back in the leather chair.

"I need to know if Mr. Abbott suspected his wife of having an affair with Sam Louis." I stared at him, waiting for an answer.

A slight smile crossed his face. Or it might have been more of a smirk. What was this man's problem?

"No, I don't think he knew what was going on." He shuffled papers on his desk and avoided my stare.

"How is that possible? If you knew, then how did he not know about this?" I asked.

Dorothy nodded as she pulled a peppermint candy from her purse and popped it into her mouth.

"Mr. Louis confided in me about their affair, but I didn't tell Mr. Abbott," he said.

"Don't you think he had a right to know?" I asked.

He frowned. "Would you have gotten involved if you were in my position? It was none of my business. I didn't want to be involved,

but Mr. Louis didn't give me that option when he told me what was going on. I insisted that he break it off, but he didn't listen to me."

"Don't you think the police should have looked more closely at Mr. Louis as a suspect instead of Allison?"

"Look, Ms. Thomas, I don't think either one of them is guilty, and I don't appreciate you coming in here and blaming Mrs. Abbott or Mr. Louis," he said.

"If you don't think Mrs. Abbott was involved, then why aren't you doing more to get her out of jail?" I crossed my arms in front of my chest.

He stood from his desk. "I think this conversation is over, Ms. Thomas. Now if you'll please leave."

He pointed toward the door as if I didn't know how to find it.

I paused for a moment before finally pushing to my feet. This wasn't the last he'd see of me.

"Come on, Dorothy. We need to leave."

She continued her death glare all the way out the door, then mumbled something under her breath as she walked past the receptionist's desk. I couldn't make out the colorful phrase for sure, but I thought she said something about her nasty disposition.

Chapter Fifteen

Dorothy decided to wait in the car while I went in to visit Allison. That was probably for the best. She'd have time to catch up on her knitting and crossword puzzles. The jail where Allison was being held was in the same location where Detective Jake Jackson worked. If there was an ounce of luck left in the world for me, I wouldn't bump into him this time.

I'd parked on the street next to a parking meter, so I knew I hadn't taken his reserved parking spot this time. There was no reason to talk to him. So why was I thinking about him the entire time I walked toward the building? I seriously needed to stop.

After stepping into the station, I waited by the front desk for someone to help me. I tapped my fingers against the counter, but no one looked my way. I stared in the officers' direction, hoping they'd sense my eyes focused on their every move. That didn't work either. Finally, I coughed loudly and caught the attention of a female officer.

I had no idea so much went into visiting an inmate. After all, I'd be separated from her by glass. Did they really have to be that thorough in their body search? I couldn't pass a cake with a file in it through the glass partition. The officer led me back to the room with the glass partitions and phones.

After a few minutes, Allison appeared from a back room. The orange jumpsuit was ugly, but somehow she made it look

good. She gave a half-hearted smile and wave as she approached. I grabbed the phone and waited for her to sit down and pick up her extension.

"How are you?" I asked as she sat down.

Of course I knew she was miserable, but I had to be polite and ask.

"As well as can be expected, I guess. I figured you'd given up on the case after I was arrested," she said.

I shook my head. "No, you hired me to do the job and that's what I intend to do."

"Do you have good news for me?" she asked with a hopeful look in her eyes.

It would be hard to tell her that I was no closer to finding the killer than when she'd first come to me. Maybe I could pick my words carefully and make the situation sound better than it actually was.

"I'm working hard on the case. I have a few leads," I said with a less-than-confident tone in my voice.

It must have worked because her eyes brightened slightly, which made me feel even worse.

"Oh yeah? Like what?" She scooted closer to the table.

I went over the leads that I had filed away in my mind. Yeah, they were minimal and pathetic.

"Have you talked to your lawyer?" I asked.

"Um, yes, we've spoken." I needed to change the subject quickly. "Is there anything else I should know? Any other leads you can give me?" I asked.

She shook her head. "I can't think of anything."

"Do you know anything about the man who owned the tower?" I asked.

"Yeah, that's a good idea. You should go talk to him." She sat up a little straighter.

"Do you know where I can find him?" I asked.

"I looked up his name, but I can't remember the exact address. I remember the street name, though," she offered.

How would I find out exactly where he lived? I couldn't drive up and down the street and hope to see him. Besides, I wasn't sure I even knew what he looked like. I'd seen him in the tower, but I wasn't positive that he was the owner of the place.

I shrugged. "I guess I can give it a shot."

Which reminded me, I had to tell Allison that I'd been shot at.

"His name is Thomas Shaw and he lives on Tropical Way," she said.

I nodded. "By the way, I went back to the condo . . . but I was shot at."

She almost dropped the phone. "What? Why would someone shoot at you? That's terrible."

"Yeah, I don't know who it was, but I wonder if it was the man who was there the day I found your husband. And if he is the owner," I said.

She paused. "There was a man? Why didn't you tell me about this? Did you tell the police?"

"I told the detective, but it was after you were arrested and he said it didn't matter. They won't even look into the matter."

"That's so typical. As far as they're concerned they've already got the killer and there's no need to look anymore," she said.

"Well, don't worry, Allison. I won't give up," I said.

"Thank you. I know I can count on you and Matt," she said.

I hated to tell her, but I didn't have much confidence in Matt Cooper. She'd find out for herself soon enough.

"What did this man at the condo look like?" she asked.

"He was tall and thin with gray hair and beady eyes," I said.

"That sounds like Mr. Shaw and it would make sense that he was there. Plus, he wanted revenge against Arthur anyway for not moving out of the building," she said.

I tapped my fingers against the table and contemplated what she'd said. He seemed like a likely suspect to me. Plus, he had a motive for killing Arthur. With Arthur dead, he could get him out of the condo like he wanted.

"I'll have to go talk to him. Although if he is the man I ran into that day, he wasn't exactly all that friendly." I frowned.

"He's not a pleasant man," she said. "So what did Matt say when you talked with him?"

"Hasn't he been by to talk with you?" I asked.

"I haven't spoken with him today, but he said he's working on getting me out of here." Her voice was full of hope.

I nodded. "Well, I didn't ask because I figured he'd already spoken to you about that, but he said that Arthur didn't know about your affair with Sam Louis," I said.

She looked down. "No, he didn't know it was Sam."

"Matt said he didn't want to be involved, so that was why he didn't tell Arthur. Matt didn't want to know what was going on between you and Louis," I said.

She shrugged. "I can understand why he wouldn't want to be involved. Matt is a no-nonsense type of man. He doesn't come off as very compassionate, but deep down I know he cares about people."

Maybe that was true, but Matt had shown me only the hard-hearted side.

"What else can you tell me about Matt?" I asked.

"Why do you want to know?" she asked suspiciously.

"I'm just trying to cover all the bases, that's all." I waved my hand dismissively.

"I can guarantee that he had nothing to do with Arthur's murder." Her expression darkened.

"Oh, I'm sure he didn't, but I was just curious as to how they got along," I said.

"They got along fine. As a matter of fact, they had dinner together the night before Arthur died," she said.

"Really? Where did they go? Do you know what they talked about?" I asked.

Maybe I'd asked one too many questions.

She frowned. "Well, I wasn't there, so I don't know what they talked about. Nothing in particular, I guess. They went to Beach Bob's on Tropical Way."

I pulled out my iPhone and typed in the name and street number for the tower owner, and then added the info about the restaurant. I'd have to stop by there and ask if anyone had overheard Arthur and Matt's conversation.

"Do you have any clue what evidence they have against you?" I asked.

Her face turned even grimmer. I hadn't thought that was possible.

"The gun used to kill him was registered to me. It had my fingerprints on it. Add that to the fact that I was having an affair and didn't have an alibi and that was all they needed. Apparently Arthur was shot in the back."

This certainly wasn't looking good for her.

"Who would have access to your gun? Where did you keep it?"

"It was at my home."

"Did anyone have access to it?" I asked.

She shrugged. "I just don't know. A few business partners of Arthur's had been over in the past few days, but I'm sure they wouldn't have taken my gun."

I had to track down whoever had gotten her gun.

"Thanks for the info," I said.

She nodded. "You'll let me know as soon as you find out anything?"

The guard approached, standing behind Allison like a tower. That was the warning that our time was up.

"Of course. You'll be the first to know." I smiled.

"Thank you," she said softly.

It was heartbreaking to leave her there.

"I'll be in touch soon," I said, then placed the receiver back on the hook.

Allison held the receiver up to her ear for a moment longer, then finally replaced it and stood. The guard escorted her away and I watched as she disappeared behind locked doors.

Since I was already at the police station, I picked up a copy of the police report, but it didn't offer any new insight. With the report in hand, I hurried across the courtyard away from the building. My mind was turning over everything that had happened. How would I find the real killer? It seemed almost impossible. What would the owner of the condo building say about Arthur Abbott? What if he was the killer? If I spoke with this man, I'd have to come to grips with the fact that I could be talking to a cold-blooded killer.

Maybe it was my imagination, but I sensed that Matt Cooper wasn't being completely forthcoming with me. He hadn't wanted to be involved with the relationship between Sam Louis and Allison. If Matt had a beef with Arthur, would he keep quiet about that too? He was representing Allison, so surely there were no hard feelings between them. He wouldn't let her sit in jail for a crime she hadn't committed, would he? Matt couldn't have killed Arthur, could he? What reason would he have to kill Arthur? He might be guilty of being a lousy lawyer at the moment, but I had no reason to believe he'd killed Arthur.

Just as I stepped onto the sidewalk, I sensed someone walking terribly close behind me. My heart rate increased. I'd left my gun in the car when I'd entered the jail. They kind of frowned upon people carrying weapons into the place to talk with prisoners. Had the killer tracked me down? I whipped around and saw a familiar face staring at me.

"You! Again!" I said, not hiding the irritation in my voice.

"What are you doing here?" Jake asked.

He wore a white button-down shirt rolled up at the forearms and black slacks. He looked more gorgeous than ever.

"What are *you* doing here?" I countered.

"Well, I work here, so..." The beginning of a smile tipped the corners of his mouth.

I crossed my arms in front of my chest. After waiting for a group of people on the sidewalk to pass us, I said, "I came here to visit my client."

"Since you're here, would you like to grab some lunch?" he asked.

I gave him a look as if he'd asked me if I wanted to kill puppies. It was probably an overreaction, huh?

"Are you kidding? Why would I want to get lunch with you? Besides, it's a little too early for lunch, don't you think?"

"Come on, you have to eat sometime. That bran muffin couldn't have gone far. You're too thin." He gestured toward my body.

"So now you're insulting me?" I asked.

He shook his head. "No, I didn't mean..."

"I have a business appointment, if you must know." I glanced at the time on my phone.

"You're not going back to the condo tower, are you?" Detective Jake Jackson looked good even when he frowned.

"What if I do?" I asked.

"I'd advise you not to do that." His gaze was fixed on me.

"Great advice, thanks. I'll keep it in mind. I want to talk with the owner of the place. Well, if I can find him." I looked over my shoulder toward my car.

He studied my face for a moment. "What if I help you find him? Will you have lunch with me then?"

I looked at him suspiciously. "Why do you want to have lunch with me anyway?"

"I like the way you wear your gun holster." He pointed.

I snorted. "That's the lamest reason I've ever heard."

He shrugged. "What can I say? It's the truth."

I released a heavy sigh. "Okay, if you help me find him I'll go to lunch with you. But I get to pick the restaurant and you're paying."

"I'm paying for the whole bill?" he asked with a smirk. "What about an appetizer?"

"We won't have time for an appetizer," I said in irritation.

"Too bad, because I could go for nachos right now." A taunting smile slid from one side of his mouth to the other.

I smirked. "How are you going to help me?"

"I know where this man is that you're looking for. I'll take you there," he offered.

"I already have his address," I said with another smirk.

That wasn't exactly the truth, but it was close enough.

"He probably won't talk to you," he said with satisfaction.

"You say that, but I have a way with people." I crossed my arms and raised an irritated eyebrow.

He laughed and the sound of his amusement softened the intensity of his gaze.

"Okay, how about I drive and you tell me where to go," I said reluctantly.

A smile crossed his lips, and to my chagrin, my stomach did a little dance.

"All right. You got a deal," he said.

"I need to drop my assistant off first. I think she has an appointment at the beauty parlor." I looked at my watch. "I can meet you back here in a couple hours."

He looked me up and down. "Don't stand me up, okay?"

I chuckled and turned on my heel. I couldn't believe that I'd agreed to have lunch with him, but if he took me to the owner of the tower, it would be worth it... maybe. When I got to my car,

I glanced back in Jake's direction. He was still watching me. He waved and my stomach flipped.

As I climbed behind the wheel, Dorothy said, "I was getting ready to come find you. My appointment is soon."

"Why do you have that smile on your face?" she asked.

I shrugged. "No reason."

She looked at me suspiciously, and then said, "What are you doing now? Would you like to come to the salon with me?"

"Dorothy, I'll be okay. You don't have to watch my every move." I offered her a reassuring smile.

"What makes you think I'm watching every move you make?" she asked.

"Ever since I was shot at you've been tagging along everywhere. I know it's not because you want to." I started the engine and shifted the gears into drive.

"I don't know what you're talking about." Dorothy continued knitting as we drove down the street.

"You aren't as clever as you think you are," I said.

"Oh yes, I am. So what if I do want to keep an eye on you? Someone needs to." She pointed the needles at me. "You don't always think things through. Just like your uncle."

She was probably right about that. I didn't always think things through. That was why I'd agreed to go to lunch with Detective Jake Jackson. If I'd thought that through, I would have turned him down.

"I can't go to the salon with you anyway. I have a lunch date." I tapped my fingers against the steering wheel as I drove.

She lowered the knitting needles and peered at me over the top of her eyeglasses. "You have a lunch date with whom? Don't tell me it's with that detective. How did that happen?"

"I don't know how it happened. It's strange ... I keep running into him everywhere," I said.

She pointed at me with a needle. "That's what I like to call fate."

To my annoyance, I felt my cheeks start to blush. "That's what I like to call bad luck."

Dorothy shook her head. "As good-looking as he is and you want to call that bad luck? I'd call you crazy for saying such a thing."

"Well, call me crazy then." I smiled widely.

Chapter Sixteen

Exhaustion had taken over by the time I rolled into the salon parking lot. Between constantly looking in the rearview mirror for strange cars and listening to Dorothy fretting about car chases, I needed a spa day. I peered up at the pink salon sign above the entrance. It was decorated with white polka dots and the words Bliss Salon printed in the middle. Maybe it wouldn't be such a bad idea after all if I went in. Maybe I could get a trim and a manicure. After all, I needed the relaxation. No, I shouldn't take the time for pampering. I needed to find a killer.

"What's on your mind, Maggie?" Dorothy asked as she gathered her things.

I waved my hand dismissively. "Oh, I thought about coming into the salon with you, but it's out of the question."

But it did look like a nice place and my bangs were in need of a trim. My nails had needed a manicure two weeks ago and I still hadn't changed the polish.

She grabbed my hand. "If you're going to lunch with that man he will see those pathetic-looking fingers while you are eating. You should come in and let Betty take care of you. She is great. She does my hair." Dorothy primped her hair with her hand.

I looked at Dorothy's gray bun and pictured myself with the same hairstyle. Hmm. I wanted to wait a few more years before

I changed my hairstyle. I glanced down at the chipped polish on my fingernails.

"Come on. It'll be good for you. After that lunatic followed us you need a break," she said.

I nodded. "Okay. I'll do it, but I don't have long before I have to meet the detective."

She wiggled her eyebrows, but I didn't acknowledge her reaction.

"Oh, but you might want to leave the gun in the car." She pointed at my Glock. "Betty has this thing where she thinks everyone is a spy and that will only reinforce the thought."

I stared at Dorothy for a second, sure that she was only kidding. "You're serious, aren't you?"

"She's just a little paranoid, but I swear she is such a good hairdresser. I just overlook it," she said breezily.

Great—this woman might turn me in for being a spy if I didn't like what she did with my hair. I forced myself out of the car and across the parking lot. Dorothy glanced back and motioned for me to hurry up. How bad could it be? I'd get the polish on my fingernails changed and maybe a little trim. I wouldn't end up with a little-old-lady haircut, right?

I took in a deep breath and stepped inside the salon. The smell of ammonia almost knocked me down. The walls were painted in the same shade of pink as the outside sign and the seating was a slightly darker shade of rose. There were several women underneath the hairdryers, a couple women in the chairs having their hair styled, and another woman getting a manicure. The women gawked at me as if I were an alien.

A woman bounced around from the back and stopped dead in her tracks when she spotted us standing by the door. She looked me up and down. I figured by the look on her face that she must be Betty and she was assessing my spy potential. She

was a short woman with bright auburn hair cut to chin length. She obviously dyed her hair because she looked to be about Dorothy's age.

When I looked around I realized that all the women appeared to be older. There was no way I was getting out of there without some kind of salon treatment. Betty stepped up to us and looked me in the eyes.

"Who have we here?" she asked.

"Betty, this is Maggie. She's my boss." Dorothy gestured toward me.

Betty quirked a brow. "So she has spy gear."

I shook my head. "No, no. I don't have spy gear." I lowered my voice, "Not on me, at least."

"Don't worry, Betty, she's fine." Dorothy waved her hand.

I prayed that the mysterious car hadn't followed us here. Betty would think the men in black had shown up.

After a long pause, she finally flashed a half-hearted smile. "What do you want done?" She looked me up and down, then said, "The works?"

Did I look like I needed the works? I glanced in one of the mirrors. Did I look that bad? I blew the bangs out of my eyes. "Maybe I'll just get a trim and a change of polish," I said.

She grabbed my hand and studied my fingernails, then looked up at me. "You need more than a polish change. What have you been doing to these cuticles? Come over here and sit down." She grabbed my arm and led me across the room.

I glanced at Dorothy and she motioned for me to go. I'd been in scary situations before. Heck, I'd even been shot at, but this was almost more terrifying than that. I plopped down into the chair and she stuffed my fingers into a bowl of sudsy water. All eyes were still on me. I must have been the youngest customer they'd had in quite some time. The manicurist didn't talk much and for that I was thankful.

After about twenty minutes, the polish on my fingers had been changed to an electric blue. I hadn't asked for the blue color, and I wasn't sure how I'd ended up with it. Apparently, the entire salon had decided that was the color for me.

"You need me to put some makeup on you?" Betty eyed me critically.

"It's Miami. How am I supposed to wear makeup? It's so hot that it'll just melt right off," I said, looking in the mirror at my bare face. Maybe I could go for a fresh coat of lip gloss and mascara.

"Oh, pish-posh. Sit down here." Betty pushed me into the chair.

Again, after about fifteen minutes, I had electric blue eye shadow on my eyelids. Two bright pink circles dotted my cheeks and red lipstick covered my lips. I hadn't seen this much makeup since I'd been to the circus. I was too afraid to say anything to Betty about the fact that I now looked like a deranged clown. Or a serial killer beauty queen.

Betty had mentioned that she wanted to pluck my eyebrows too. There was no way I would allow that to happen. That was where I drew the line.

"You look really pretty. I love that shade of blue," a woman under the nearest hair dryer said.

The other women nodded in unison. In reality, the truth was that I looked ridiculous. What would Jake think? I'd probably scare him away. Hey, maybe this was how I could finally get him to stop following me. One look at my clown makeup would scar him for life.

"Can you tell us more about your job?" the hairdresser beside me asked.

I looked at Betty and wondered how much information I should share. Dorothy was under the hair dryer so she wouldn't be there to tell me when I'd gone too far.

Finally I said, "Well, I'm a private investigator. I usually just offer discreet investigations for cheating spouses, that sort of thing."

They didn't need to know that I was working on my very first case ever. What would they think if I told them it was a murder investigation?

"That sounds exciting and so dangerous," the woman getting her hair butchered said.

They didn't know the half of it.

"I bet you get a lot of cheating husbands," the woman said as she shook her head.

The hair stylist pulled the scissors away before she cut a chunk of the woman's hair off.

Visions of having chunks of my own hair whacked off ran through my head. Attempting not to worry about the hairstyling disaster waiting to happen, I continued the conversation as a distraction. "Actually, the last case I had was a woman cheating on her husband."

The women shook their heads.

"Such a shame. Did you catch her in the act?" Betty asked.

I grinned. "Yes, I did."

"I have a woman who comes in here who is cheating on her husband. She tells me all about it. It's more information than I want, but I just listen. It's not my place to tell her not to do it," Betty said.

I dodged the makeup brush as she attempted to add more blush. "I can understand why you wouldn't want to know."

"What case are you working on now?" Betty asked.

I wasn't sure if I should share that information. "Um, it's a death investigation." I lowered my voice.

The room stopped and they stared at me.

Betty's eyes widened. "Who was killed?"

They all stared waiting for an answer. I'd already said too much and I needed to change the subject.

I shifted in my seat. "I'm afraid I can't give out that information."

"It sounds so official," the woman said.

Betty was looking at me suspiciously the whole time I was talking. The more I talked the more convinced she looked that I was a spy.

When Betty brought out the scissors, I had a flash of Edward Scissorhands and I couldn't handle it anymore. I had to get out of there while I still had hair.

I jumped up from the seat. "You know, I just remembered that I have something else I need to do before I meet my appointment." I walked toward the front of the salon.

"But you look so pretty," Dorothy said. "Why don't you let her finish?"

"Yes, she did a great job, but nonetheless this can't be avoided."

"So you're sure you have a ride home, Dorothy?" I asked as I walked backwards toward the door.

If she said she didn't have a ride and that I needed to hang around, I'd let her have it. She must have noticed the stern look in my eyes because she nodded.

"Yes, I have a ride. Thank you." A small smile touched her lips.

I placed cash on the counter. "Thanks again, Betty. You did a lovely job."

My voice wavered and I wondered if she knew I was fibbing. How would I get this makeup off before I met Jake? I'd need a chisel.

Betty snapped the scissors. "You sure you don't want that trim? It'll only take a couple minutes."

"No, I'm good." I waved my hands through the air.

When I finally made it out of the salon and to my car, movement from across the parking lot caught my attention. For a brief

moment, I thought it was Allison Abbott. She had the same shade of blonde hair, cut in the same style. It looked just like her. But then I realized she was still in jail and I hadn't done a darn thing to get her out.

As the woman moved closer, I could see more clearly that it wasn't Allison. The woman looked at me and nodded, then continued into the salon. I wanted to warn her. Tell her to get out while she still had a chance. Didn't she know what she was getting herself into as soon as she stepped inside that building?

Before one of the women changed their mind about letting me escape, I jumped into my car and headed for my lunch appointment. I definitely wouldn't call it a date. As I headed down the palm tree-lined street, my phone rang, so I pulled over to take the call. Something had come up with Detective Jackson and our non-date had been cancelled.

Of course he wouldn't tell me what had come up, but I knew by the police scanner app on my iPhone that police had been called to the condo tower again. Detective Jackson would have to wake up a lot earlier if he wanted to try a fast one on me. I pointed my car in the direction of the condo tower, intent on finding out what had happened.

Chapter Seventeen

When I pulled up to the building, police were swarming the area. I had to park my car far away. Unfortunately, it didn't look as if I'd be able to get close to the condos. I decided to walk as close as I could get until the police stopped me. People had gathered near the building and stood on the sidewalk watching the activity. Maybe I could blend in with the crowd and Jake wouldn't notice that I was there. I approached a group of people and acted as if I had no idea what was going on.

"What happened?" I asked the little old lady standing beside me.

"I heard gunshots, but I don't know. I hope no one was injured." She shook her head.

I nodded. "Yeah, me too."

Of course, police tape marked off the area so that no one could enter the scene. If I hadn't thought I'd be shot, I'd have just slipped right under there. Police ran back and forth as if they didn't have a clue what was going on either. At least I didn't feel quite as left out now.

The woman had said that she'd heard gunshots. I'd listened to the police scanner, but I wasn't familiar with the codes, so I wasn't sure what had happened. It wasn't like I could walk up to the cops and ask them. They'd tell me to mind my own business. I pulled out my book of police lingo and referenced the code that I'd heard

on the scanner. I flipped through it and found the code I was looking for. Sure enough, it was for a shooting. Since there was no ambulance around I assumed no one had been hurt. That was one good thing in this situation.

How would I find out exactly what had happened? The best that I could think of at the moment was to walk over to the sectioned-off area and try to eavesdrop on the police who were talking to each other. I casually moved closer to the area. An officer fixed his gaze on me and frowned. He probably knew that I wanted to snoop around. Don't ask me how he knew, but he knew. It was probably written all over my face. Maybe Jake had passed around my picture at the police station. I smiled at the officer, but his stony expression didn't change. So much for using my charms on him.

As I nonchalantly walked around the area, I spotted Jake standing next to another officer. They were engrossed in conversation. Jake looked so handsome in the afternoon sunlight. What was I thinking? *Focus on the task at hand*, I reminded myself. It wasn't important how handsome he looked.

Jake must have felt my stare because he looked over. Our eyes met. There was no way he hadn't seen me. Could I dash away and make him believe that he'd only imagined seeing me? Yeah, that was a highly improbable scenario. When he turned and hurried in my direction, I spun around.

I headed back toward my car, rushing my steps. I'd never been a fast walker. As I made it past the entrance landscaping, I thought about hopping behind the shrubbery and trying to hide. Chances were pretty high that he'd spot me right away. When he set his sights on something, he didn't let go. He had a laser-like focus. I heard his footsteps as he closed the distance between us. I didn't turn around, though. Maybe if I ignored him, he would leave me alone. I felt his presence behind me. In my mind I went over possible excuses to give him. It was doubtful he would believe

any of them. Anything I came up with sounded ridiculous to me, so I knew it would to him too.

Someone grabbed my arm. I knew who it was before I even spun around. I sucked in a deep breath and faced Jake Jackson.

"Maggie Thomas, what are you doing here? You couldn't stand to be away from me for another minute, huh?" he asked.

I narrowed my eyes at him. "You think you're so clever." I straightened. "You know why I'm here. Something happened, didn't it? You can't hide these things from me," I said, proud of myself for finding out about the incident.

He ran his hand through his hair. "I suppose I can't hide things from you. You're good."

Okay, now he was just mocking me. "See, I am right. There is something going on here and it's related to the murder. You can try to hide this from me all you want, but I plan on getting to the bottom of it," I said.

"Yes, there was a shooting here today," he said.

"Another shooting," I corrected him.

"Yes, another shooting. We don't know that they're related," he said.

"Oh, come on. You can't expect me to believe that."

He smiled at my bluntness.

"A madman has a gun and apparently is targeting this building. What are you all going to do? Just keep ignoring the facts?" I said.

"We're doing our job. You have a job to do and so do I," he said matter-of-factly.

I spun around to walk away and he matched my pace, walking beside me.

"Where are you going, Thomas?" he asked.

I didn't look over at him because I didn't want to see his sexy smile right now. I was mad and I intended to stay that way for at least five minutes.

"Are you ready to get some lunch now?" he asked, with a devilish tone in his voice.

"No, I am not ready for lunch," I said.

"Oh, come on, Thomas," he said.

"Stop calling me that," I said.

"It's your name, right?" he asked with a smile.

"Yes, but you can call me—oh, never mind," I said.

"What are you going to do about the residents here? They're scared," I said, as I pointed to the group of people huddled together outside the front gate.

"We have police who are going to watch the building," he said.

We'd reached my car.

"Thank you for the info, Jackson," I said as I opened the car door.

"You're welcome," he said.

When I looked at him he flashed that dazzling smile. My five minutes weren't up, so I couldn't return the smile.

"I'll call you later," he said as I closed the door.

I smirked as I drove away. When I looked in the rearview mirror, he was still watching my car as I drove away.

I left the scene of the crime and pointed my car toward my apartment. I was halfway home as I bit back a smile. Yes, my five minutes were up.

Chapter Eighteen

The next day everything would have been fine if not for the same black vehicle following Dorothy and me again. My world was spinning out of control.

"Dorothy, the black car is following us again," I said.

She lifted her spectacles up on her face, peered in the rearview mirror, and then said, "Well, I'll be damned."

"What the hell do they want?" My heart rate increased. "Do you think it's the same man who was in the SUV?"

"Punch it." Dorothy reached over and pushed down on my leg, making my foot hit the gas pedal even harder.

We lurched forward. It was a good thing no other cars were in front of us.

"What are you doing?" I yelled.

"This is life or death. It calls for desperate measures," she said in all seriousness.

I knew a trick that I'd seen on one of the detective shows (which one failed me at the moment, but that was neither here nor there), but what were the odds that I'd be able to pull it off in real life? Besides, it had probably been a fake stunt anyway. What did I have to lose at this point, though? I stepped on the gas again, without Dorothy's help this time. I steered the car onto the next street, then immediately pulled into the parking garage. The only problem with my plan, though, was that the parking

garage was closed. The gate didn't lift and I was stuck at the guard stand.

"What are you going to do now?" Dorothy asked in a panicked tone.

"I don't know. Let me think," I said.

"Well, you'd better think of something fast," she said.

To my surprise, when I looked in the rearview mirror, the black car zoomed past. I held my breath, waiting for it back up, but that never happened. Had they really not seen my car sitting there? I couldn't get that lucky. How would I get out of here? I'd have to back up and pull out onto the street again. I'd have to do it quickly, though, before the car came back and trapped me in this spot. I shifted into reverse and tapped the gas lightly. After another car had passed, I pulled back onto the street. Up ahead, I spotted the black car. It was parked on the side of the road. Unfortunately, it was too far away to read the license plate number. I couldn't drive past, so I pulled over to the curb.

After a couple seconds, the car merged back into traffic and I zipped in right behind it. I was going to find out who this person was and what he wanted.

"What are you doing?" Dorothy asked.

"We're following him."

After a few blocks, the car turned into a gym parking lot. I circled the lot and found a spot. Dorothy hopped out behind me as we followed the man toward the building.

We rushed through the gym doors, ready to confront the man who had followed us. But once inside, I stopped in my tracks.

"Which one is he?" Dorothy asked, adjusting her eyeglasses again.

The space was jam-packed with men. Their biceps were as big as my head. They wore loose-fitting pants that resembled pajamas and tank tops that looked like they were about three sizes too

small. Apparently they wanted to show off their top halves and hide the bottom half. Loud music blared from overhead speakers. Bangs and clanks from the weights being hoisted up and slammed down filled the air. There was also quite a bit of grunting going on.

"How are we going to find him?" I asked.

"I think we're the only women in the place." Dorothy pointed out.

"I can see that," I said.

"What was he wearing?" she asked.

I glared at her. "He was wearing the pajama pants and a tank top combo that seems to be so popular. Apparently, that's the bodybuilder uniform for this place."

The smell of sweat and dirty socks lingered in the air. Shining weight bars filled with weights were lined up as far as the eye could see.

"Wait. Is that him?" She pointed at a muscle man at the back of the room.

I peered across the room. The mirrors lining each wall made it appear like there were a thousand times more beefed-up men. We were surrounded by them, like clowns in a fun-house mirror.

"Yeah, I think that's him. Let's go after him. He'll see how it feels to be followed," I said, gesturing for Dorothy to follow me.

As we made our way across the gym, the man was leaving through a back exit. Where was he going? He'd just gotten there, and I was pretty sure that he hadn't seen us follow him in.

As he walked out the back door, he accidentally dropped his fanny pack. I picked up my pace, but it was no use. He'd disappeared out the back door.

"If we hurry maybe we can catch him," I said.

We reached the door, but when I opened it and peered around the back alley, the man was nowhere in sight.

"I think we lost him," I said with frustration.

Others were staring at us now. I guessed we did look a bit out of place in this building. I reached down and picked up the bag before someone else could snatch it. A couple guys beside me frowned, but there was no way they were getting that bag from me . . . muscles or no.

"Come on. Let's get out of here," I said, motioning for Dorothy to follow.

As we walked across the gym floor, a guy stepped out in front of us. He looked as if his head was much too small for his body thanks to the inflated muscles. His blond hair was cut in a mullet—business on top and party in the back.

"Hey, doll, you looking for a trainer?" He smiled.

Maybe my biceps were a little too soft and my butt could stand to be a tad, okay a lot, tighter, but there was no way I wanted a personal trainer. If I wanted to torture myself I'd stop eating chocolate . . . although, now that I thought about it, maybe coming to the gym wouldn't be a bad idea. If I came back, I might find the guy who had followed me and find out what he wanted.

"Yeah, I guess I could tone up a little," I said.

He looked me up and down. If he agreed with that statement, I might kick him in the shin. It wasn't like I never exercised. I ran on the beach all the time. Okay, not all the time, but a couple times a week over to the bakery for a bear claw.

"I have reasonable rates and I'll make sure to really work you over," he said.

Dorothy made a gagging noise. I stepped in front of her before she reached out and smacked the guy with her big brown pocketbook.

"Why don't you give me your business card and I can give you a call," I said.

"Oh, I don't have any cards, but I'd be happy to write my number down for you. My name's Erich Cochran," he said.

Some business he had. Even I had business cards. I'd had some made with a cute magnifying glass and my name underneath. I thought the three shades of pink on the cards really made them pop.

"How about I just type your number into my phone?" I pulled it from my pocket and poised my finger over the screen.

He ran his large hand through his short spiky blond hair. "Yeah, that'll work."

He rattled off his number as I tapped the screen on my phone.

"Okay. I got it. Thanks. I'll give you a call," I said.

"Yeah, great. I'm looking forward to working you out," he said.

Again Dorothy picked up her pocketbook as if she was about to take a swipe at him. I grabbed her arm and guided her away.

I waved my hand over my shoulder as we walked away. I knew he was staring at us as we left. He was probably staring at my saggy butt, the jerk.

As we neared the front of the gym, a guy running on a treadmill looked down at his shoelace, then fell forward onto the treadmill, zooming back off the thing and landing on the floor. No one else appeared to notice the ruckus. If they did, they didn't care because they continued pumping out their reps. The guy had totally crashed and burned.

Dorothy and I ran over as he lifted himself from the floor. He had dark hair and was about half the size of the other men in the building. He also didn't wear their standard uniform, but instead had on gray shorts and a blue T-shirt. Apparently, he had gotten away from taking their oath. Lucky him.

"Are you okay?" I asked.

"You poor dear, you just about knocked your teeth out," Dorothy said.

He gave an embarrassed, lopsided grin. "I'm fine. Thanks for your concern."

I studied his face for a moment. "If you're sure."

He nodded. "I'm fine." He grabbed his water bottle and towel. "Thank you, ladies." He waved and walked away.

"He seems out of place here," Dorothy said.

I stared in his wake. "Yes, he does. Not to mention he looked really familiar. Where do I know him from?"

"Well, it's certainly not from the gym," she quipped.

"No, but I've seen him before," I said.

"You're not going to let that Erich guy instruct you on fitness, are you?" Dorothy asked with a frown.

"I thought maybe it would be a good idea to have an excuse to come back and look for the guy who's following us," I said.

She frowned for a moment, then finally relented and agreed with my genius idea. "I guess that is a good idea, but don't get too muscular."

"I don't think we have anything to worry about in that department," I said.

She looked me up and down. "You are kind of skinny. Maybe you should order extra on your lunch date with Jake."

"I don't have a lunch date and I have plenty of meat on my bones, thank you," I said.

"Well, if you don't have a lunch date then you should. And you're right about the meat on your bones. It's all in the rump area." She wiggled her finger in the direction of my butt.

I glared at her. "Dorothy, you'd better watch what you say or your knitting needles might accidentally fall into the Dumpster."

"I don't find that funny, dear."

When we finally made it out of the gym, I climbed into the car with our found treasure still in my hand. At least I'd come out of there with something.

"What do you think is in that ugly thing, anyway?" Dorothy asked.

"I don't know. I feel like I'm looking into the guy equivalent of a purse," I said.

"And don't forget the kitchen sink. Just open the darn thing." She pointed.

I unzipped it and whispered, "I don't know, but I'm about to find out. We shouldn't be doing this, huh?"

"You have to find the owner, right?" She winked. "So go ahead and open it up."

"Right." I nodded, then unzipped the bag before I chickened out.

"What's in it?" Dorothy asked like an impatient child.

I began removing the contents: an empty package of gum, two crumpled-up dollar bills, a pen and paper, a chocolate-flavored condom, and bubble gum-flavored lip balm. I noticed a piece of paper and pulled it from the depths of the bag. Actually, it looked like a page torn out of a magazine. It had been folded twice. I unfolded it, then immediately wished that I hadn't. Don't get me wrong, I enjoy the male physique . . . very much so, but this guy was creepy.

"Eww," I said.

"What is it?" Dorothy asked, grabbing it from my hands.

"Don't look. You'll want to remove your eyes with your knitting needles," I said.

"Well, he's certainly not bashful, is he?" she said, staring at the picture.

The guy was carrying around a nude picture of himself? Apparently, *Playgirl* magazine had published his picture. He probably used it to hit on potential dates.

"Get rid of that thing," I said.

Dorothy folded the magazine clipping back up and tossed it into the car's middle console. "What else you got in there?" she asked.

"I don't want to stick my hand in there again," I said.

"You have to. There might be an ID in there with his name on it. It's your job." She smiled.

I thought she was getting a little too much pleasure out of this. Finally, she leaned over and peered into the bag. "What's 'extra ribbed' mean?"

I remained speechless. There was no way I was schooling Dorothy on condoms today.

"Oh, dear." Her eyes widened. "For pleasure," she said under her breath.

"I told you I don't want to stick my hand in there," I said.

She sucked in a deep breath, then said, "I'll do it."

Dorothy snatched the bag from me and stuffed her hand in. In one swift movement, she pulled out the still-wrapped condom. Then she pulled out a small bottle of jasmine-scented lotion and some peppermint-flavored breath mints.

"Is there any identification?" I asked, leaning over to get a look.

"I don't see anything with a name on it," she said.

"What a waste of time. Now what are we going to do with the bag?" I asked.

She stuffed the contents back into it, barely touching the condom as she tossed it in. "Well, you could take it back in there and tell them you found it."

I thought throwing it into a trash can seemed like a better option, but I would feel bad for doing it. Yeah, I was too much of a softy. I mean, the guy had been following me. He deserved to lose his bag.

"Fine. I'll take it back," I said, grabbing the bag and climbing out of the car again.

I hoped I didn't run into the muscle guy again. But then I thought about the other guy. The one who seemed out of place and as if he had no idea why he was there or what he was doing. If only I could remember where I'd seen him before. Since I was new in town, it wasn't like there were that many options. I really needed to get out more.

The guy behind the counter took the bag when I handed it to him, but he seemed less than interested. He wanted to get back to his bodybuilder magazine.

"Do you happen to know who owns this bag?" I asked.

He looked me up and down, then muttered, "Nope." He looked back down at the magazine.

"Yeah, thanks for the help," I said sarcastically.

Chapter Nineteen

I shouldn't have answered his call, but temporary insanity had taken over my mind. Jake called and asked me to meet him for lunch. I'd agreed, but only if he promised to take me to the condo owner's home. As I headed over to pick up Jake, I couldn't help but repeatedly glance in my rearview mirror for the meathead from the gym.

Why had Jake offered to take me to the condo owner, anyway? What was in it for him? I knew it wasn't just because he wanted to go to lunch with me. The car seemed quiet without the clacking of Dorothy's knitting needles. It was nice to have the time to think things through. One thing was for sure, I needed to come up with a better plan. If the tower owner was the killer, then who was the guy from the gym? And more importantly, what did he want with me? I had no choice but to go back to that gym. I wasn't looking forward to having that musclehead making my muscles burn. This hadn't been in the job description when I'd thought about being a private investigator.

Within a few minutes I had Jake in my car and was pulling up in front of an address that Jake claimed was Thomas Shaw's home.

"How do you know where this guy lives?" I asked.

"The man has called the police a few times," Jake said.

"Why has he called the police so many times?" I asked.

He looked out the window. "Different reasons ..."

"You're not giving me all the details. Come on, spill it," I said.

"I will admit he's had disagreements in the past with Arthur Abbott," he said.

"I knew it. See, that's the kind of stuff you should have told me right away," I said.

I parked the car and Jake and I walked up the driveway and knocked on the front door.

"Is Thomas Shaw available?" I asked when a woman answered the door.

I was surprised how much she reminded me of Allison, with the same blonde hair and bright smile. She looked me up and down and then shifted her focus to Jake. She didn't appear happy about the fact that we were standing on her front porch.

She gave Jake a dramatic stare from under lashes that were so long and thick they cast shadows on her cheeks. "He's not home right now. May I tell him who was calling?"

"Miami Police," Jake said before I had a chance to respond.

He whipped out his badge and flashed it at her. I had to admit, that was kind of sexy.

I'd wanted to do all the talking, but this woman would probably respond to the police more than she would me, so I let it slide.

She inched the door closed a little and said, "I'll make sure to tell him you were here."

With that, she shut the door completely, leaving us standing there staring at the faux boxwood wreath under the knocker.

"It seems like she was in a hurry to get rid of us," I said.

Jake scowled. "It does appear that way, doesn't it?"

I smirked. "Why would she do that, unless . . ."

"That doesn't exactly mean that her husband—or whoever he is to her—is guilty of murder," he said.

I held my hands up in surrender. "I didn't say that it did, just that it's a little odd."

"People don't usually invite the police in for milk and cookies," he said.

We stood in the driveway for a moment. I felt eyes on me so I looked back up at the house. The woman was standing at the window staring down at us. When she saw me watching her, she shut the blinds.

"Who do you think she is? The wife?" I asked.

"I'm not sure if he's married. If it's not his wife, it must be his girlfriend," Jake said as he opened the passenger door of my car. "You ready for lunch?"

"What? We haven't found him yet," I said.

"You promised we'd go to lunch," he said.

"You promised we'd find the owner," I said.

"I said I would take you to his house. I didn't guarantee that he'd be here." He smirked.

"You're not getting away with that. I need to ask this man questions." I buckled my seat belt, then turned the key in ignition. "We're going to the tower to look for him."

"What exactly do you plan to ask this man?" he asked.

"Well, for starters I want to ask what problem he had with Arthur. I mean, I know he wanted him to move, but was it really that big of an issue? Would it be enough to push him to kill Arthur? If this is the same man who I saw that day at the tower, then I know he's guilty," I said as I navigated the streets back toward the tower.

"I'd hate to have you as a juror if I was on trial," he said.

"As long as you don't do anything wrong I guess you won't have anything to worry about," I said.

"Why do you want to get Allison out of jail, anyway?" he asked.

"You still haven't figured that out by now?" I asked.

"No, I guess I haven't," he said.

"She paid me money to find the killer. It's my case. Besides, I don't think she did it. So as far as I can tell, it's the right thing to do," I said.

"Is that right?" He tapped his finger against the seat.

I was almost afraid to find out what he was thinking. I knew he was about to let me know what was on his mind.

"So tell me, Maggie, P.I., what do you do for fun? Besides chasing down killers and dodging bullets?" he asked with a smile.

Did I dare tell him I liked to watch reruns of detective shows in my spare time? No way. He didn't need more ammunition to think I was incompetent.

"Well, I like to read and run on the beach, and I also like to paint," I said.

I cringed when I realized that it sounded like I was reading him my singles ad.

"What do you paint?" he asked, as if he was genuinely interested.

Taking one hand off the steering wheel, I waved it dismissively. "I'll paint whatever I see that sparks my creative side. Sometimes it's a beach scene, sometimes a still life."

"I'd love to see your work," he said.

"Enough about me, though. What do you do when you're not arresting innocent people?" I asked.

He frowned. "Hey, that was a cheap shot."

"Sorry," I said. "I know you don't always arrest innocent people, but in this one case I think you got it wrong."

"Duly noted," he said. He ran his hand through his hair, "Well, when I'm not working I like to run on the beach and read…" I glanced over at him. Was he just repeating what I'd said? "I also play the guitar."

I quirked a brow. "Really?"

"You seem surprised. Is that a shock?" he asked.

"No. not at all. What type of music do you play?" I asked.

"A little bit of everything. I like it all," he said.

"But what is your favorite?" I asked.

"That's a tough question. Maybe classic rock," he said.

I nodded. "I like that music too." It wasn't my favorite, but I listened on occasion.

I pulled the car up to the curb and shoved the gearshift into park.

"Doesn't this place seem creepy now that it's abandoned?" I said, looking over at the tall, empty building.

He stared for a second. "Yeah, I guess it is a little lonely."

I took the keys out of the ignition and opened the door. "Come on. Let's see if we can find him."

"Are you going to interrogate the man? Are you going to ask him if he killed Arthur Abbott?" he asked with a smirk.

"Maybe. It's worth a shot," I said. "I've seen it work on TV shows before."

Oops. I hadn't meant to mention that. I couldn't let him in on my dirty little rerun secret.

His eyes widened. "That's the only place it works."

I ignored his comment and continued toward the building. Luckily, since Jake was with me, I didn't have to look around before I slipped under the police scene tape. He held it up for me as I crossed under it.

"Thanks," I said softly.

"You're welcome." He stared at my face for longer than I was comfortable with, so I shifted my attention toward the building.

He cleared his throat. "Well, I think it's safe to say that he's not here either."

"We don't know that for sure. We haven't even looked inside yet," I said.

"His car isn't here." Jake gestured around the empty lot.

I looked to my left. "Maybe he's in the other building."

Jake shielded his eyes with his hand and peered across at the other tall condo tower. "Okay, I'll bite. Let's take a look, but if we don't find him there, I'm afraid I'll have to insist on lunch."

I bit my lip to keep from smiling. I had to keep up the professional façade. "Fine. If he isn't there we can get food. You must eat a lot."

"I eat. Apparently that's not something you want to do," he said.

My stomach rumbled and an image of those previously mentioned nachos flashed in my mind. "Oh, I eat plenty." I marched toward the building, leaving Jake standing in the same spot.

The parking lot of this condo tower was mostly empty too. "There aren't a lot of cars at this one either. What's the deal?" I asked.

"I don't think they were able to sell many condos in either tower. That's why people moved to this one," he said.

When we stepped into the building's lobby, a woman greeted us as she walked toward the elevator. Her pink flip-flops made a *swoosh* noise as she stepped across the tile. She had a giant straw tote bag draped over her shoulder and a white swimsuit cover-up that reached to her knees. Dark hair sprinkled with gray peeked out from under her straw hat.

"Oh, hello, Detective Jackson, it's nice to see you. Is everything okay?" she asked, with concern in her eyes.

The residents were probably on edge since Arthur's body had been discovered.

"No, nothing's wrong, Mrs. Page. Have you seen Thomas Shaw?" Jake asked as I stepped over to the back entrance.

I figured I'd give him a moment to speak with the woman and possibly find Mr. Shaw's location. I wondered how Jake knew this woman. I'd have to ask later.

The glass door led out to the patio where there was a large turquoise pool and white wicker loungers; beyond that lay the ocean. It was odd to see the beach mostly empty. But as I looked out the window, I noticed something in the water straight ahead. What was it? A float? A shark?

Jake was still talking to the resident, so I stepped out the back door for a better look. Waves of heat assaulted me and I longed to dive into the sparkling pool.

As I stood on the pool patio, straining to see, I still couldn't make out what was in the ocean. I slipped off my favorite white sandals with the blue flowers attached to the top and headed out across the sand. It was hot under my feet at first, but then I hit the cooler part where the water had previously been.

As I neared the water, I stopped in my tracks. My heart raced and I couldn't believe what I was seeing. A body was face down on the shore. I looked to my left and right and saw a few people down the beach, but no one was nearby.

When I glanced back, I spotted Jake on the pool patio. He threw up his hand. Obviously he couldn't see what I saw. I waved my hands through the air to show a sign of distress, then I took off running toward Jake.

He met me half way with a frown on his face. "What's wrong?"

"There's a body in the water," I said breathlessly.

"What?" He glanced over my shoulder. "You're kidding," he said as he took off running down the beach.

I quickly followed behind him. When I reached the body again, Jake had already pulled out his cell phone and was talking to what I assumed were his fellow police officers. Jake must have turned the body over because now I saw the man's bloated face. I was sure I recognized him right away.

"That's the man who was here the day Arthur was murdered." I looked plaintively at Jake.

"That's the owner of this building, Mr. Shaw," Jake said as he shoved his phone back into his pocket.

My mouth dropped. I knew it. My instincts had been right—the man had been Thomas Shaw. People had started to gather around by the time the police arrived. They probably wondered why two people were standing over a dead body.

While the police inspected the crime scene, I stepped back into the pool area and watched the action. I sat on one of the loungers and tried to wrap my mind around what had happened. If this man was dead, then who had killed Arthur? Had he killed Arthur, then been murdered too? I had suspected that he had killed him, but now I would never know. Now I had another mystery on my hands. Who had killed Thomas Shaw? Was his death connected in any way to Arthur Abbott's? It had to be, right? Two people murdered in the same area. Well, I was getting ahead of myself; I wasn't sure that Thomas Shaw had been murdered. But I was pretty darn sure because it looked as if he had a bullet hole in his chest.

"How are you?" Jake asked as he approached.

"I'm doing okay," I said as I ran a hand through my hair.

"I'll probably be here for a little while longer. You should go get lunch," he said.

I shook my head. "I'm not sure I'm very hungry after finding him."

He nodded. "That's understandable."

I pushed to my feet. "I can wait around if you need a ride." I motioned over my shoulder toward the street.

He smiled softly. "I'd like that, but like I said, I'll be a while. I wouldn't want you to wait around. I can catch a ride with one of the other detectives."

I nodded. "Okay. Well, thanks . . . for your help."

I walked toward the door. I knew he was still watching me. After a few more steps, I turned around. "You do know that this murder is connected to Arthur Abbott's, right?"

He looked me in the eyes and said, "I can't say that for sure."

I let out a deep breath, then turned on my heel and walked away. This time I didn't look back. I knew he had a job to do, but so did I. Now I just needed to prove to him that I was right.

Chapter Twenty

I stepped back into the tower, crossing through the foyer and toward the door.

"Is something going on out there?" The woman who had been in the lobby before spoke to me as she craned her neck to look over my shoulder. "I saw all the police cars."

I had hoped I would get out of there before anyone asked me questions. No such luck. "There was a bit of an incident," I said glancing back at the door. "Someone is dead."

She gasped as her hand flew up to her mouth. "Did someone drown on the beach?"

Considering the man was fully clothed, I had a feeling he hadn't gone for a dip. "I'm not sure what happened at this point, but yes, he was in the water," I said.

She shook her head. "When will they learn that the water can be dangerous? They get sucked out in the rip current and don't know how to get out."

"Yes, well, I must be going now." I pointed toward the door.

She grabbed my arm on my way toward the door. "Do you know who it was?"

She was just full of questions. I wasn't about to tell her who it was, although now that I thought about it, I wondered if she'd seen anything suspicious.

I turned around to face her. "I don't know who it is," I lied.

"That's simply awful," she said as she twisted her hands together.

"By the way, did you see anything unusual today?" I asked.

She frowned. "What do you mean 'unusual'?"

I shrugged. "I don't know... anyone hanging around who shouldn't have been? Maybe they were acting strange?"

She scrunched her face in concentration. "I can't think of anything." She held her index finger up. "Wait. There was one thing."

My eyes widened. "Yes?"

"The owner of the building was here in the lobby arguing with a man." She looked as if a light bulb had gone off. She had just figured out that I wanted her to share the details. "Oh, he's the man who owns the buildings. Well, I say *owns*, but he has other partners. We've never seen the other partners, though, just him. I guess they just provide the money."

Bingo. I froze. What good fortune that I'd gotten this information before the cops had. Yes! What I would do with it I wasn't sure, but just the fact that I'd gotten it first was pretty good in my book.

"He was here today talking with someone, but who? Do you know the man he was speaking with?" I asked.

"Um, no I can't say that I do know who he was." She smiled as if to say she was truly sorry.

"Do you know what he looked like?" I asked.

She waved her hand. "Oh, he had graying hair. Average height and weight."

Well, that didn't tell me much. There were plenty of people around matching that description. "Did you overhear what they were talking about?" I asked.

She scowled. "I'm not in the habit of eavesdropping on other people's conversations."

"No, I didn't think you'd do it on purpose. I just thought perhaps you'd overheard something."

She looked down at her feet. "Well, I may have heard something." Her voice lowered. "The man was demanding money and the owner said that someone should have done the job himself if he hadn't been happy with the way it turned out."

I had no idea what I would do with this information, but I knew it was big and it meant something.

"Thanks for everything," I said as I hurried to the door.

After leaving the condo tower, I headed home. More than anything, I needed a shower and time to think about everything. My lunch and dinner had consisted of a peanut butter sandwich and a margarita while sitting on the sofa and watching *Magnum P.I.* Yeah, it wasn't exactly the best combination. I really needed to improve my nutritional intake. But in my defense, after discovering two bodies, I really felt the margarita was necessary. I'd gotten one of the bottled mixes with the tequila already added in. It took too much time to mix them up from scratch.

Later that evening, my phone rang. I scrambled up from the sofa, where I'd fallen asleep, tripped on the rug, and then finally reached the phone.

"Maggie here," I answered.

I'd decided that answering the phone by announcing my first name sounded like a great private eye kind of thing to do.

A chuckle sounded from the other end and I knew immediately who was calling.

"How's it going, Maggie, P.I.?" Jake asked.

He was up to something. I could tell by the tone of his voice.

"Why do you want to know?" I asked suspiciously.

"Good job today. You got to the witness before we did," he said.

So he'd talked with the resident. "You win some, you lose some," I said with satisfaction. "Just trying to do my job."

"Are you doing okay?" he asked.

"I had a margarita," I said.

He chuckled. "So I guess you are doing better now."

"I'll make it. Thanks for calling," I said.

"I'll see you around, Maggie, P.I.," he said in a teasing tone and then clicked off the phone.

Chapter Twenty-One

When I walked through the door, I was surprised to see Dorothy already at her desk. And even more shocking, she didn't have her knitting needles. However, her hair was poofier than normal. I was glad I hadn't stayed around the salon longer or my hair would have turned out in the same style. I wasn't looking forward to explaining to Dorothy how I'd found another dead guy.

She tapped her fingers against the wood of her desk. "I can't leave you alone for two seconds." She held up the newspaper.

A picture of the beach with a ton of people standing around was splashed on the front page with the headline "Body Found on the Shore." The worst part of the photo was that I was at the crime scene with Jake. It would be impossible to deny my way out of this one.

I set my purse and gun down on my desk. "Oh yeah, that." I waved my hand dismissively.

She glared. "Don't act all nonchalant with me. It says right here in the paper that you found the body. That's two bodies you've found." She held up two fingers.

"Well, it was just a coincidence," I said.

"I don't think it's a coincidence that two people were murdered there at that condo," she said.

"How do you know that he was murdered?" I had my suspicions, but still.

She tapped the newspaper and handed it to me. "I know it was murder because it says so right here on the page."

That changed everything for sure. I had to find out who Mr. Shaw had been talking to before his murder. I knew it was related to Arthur's murder—call it a hunch.

The morning had been a long one. I'd spent time going over every clue I'd found. I wrote out a list of all the information that I'd collected so far. Yes, the list was short; that was why the morning had dragged on and on.

When the phone rang, Dorothy and I stared at each other in shock. Yeah, I didn't get a lot of calls, but with any luck that would change in the future. Finally, after a pause, she answered it. She motioned for me to pick up the phone.

The entire time I talked with the woman on the other end of the line, Dorothy stared at me. She might as well have picked up her line and eavesdropped. It would have been easier. Surprisingly, I'd gotten a call for another case.

When I hung up the phone, Dorothy demanded to know who it was. "Was it about the murders?" she asked with enthusiasm.

"A simple cheating spouse case," I said.

I paused and looked at her. "Yeah, maybe the cheating spouse cases aren't so simple after all."

"Well, let's hope it doesn't turn out like the last one," she said.

"If it turns up with another dead body, then I am getting out of the business," I said.

"Good idea." She waved her hand.

I tapped a pen against the blank legal pad as I contemplated my next move. I'd woken up with a plan, but I hadn't quite pulled the trigger on it. Now was that time.

"Dorothy, I'm stepping out for lunch," I said as I picked up my bag and gun.

She grabbed her giant pocketbook. "Not without me, you don't."

"What? I'll be fine, Dorothy. I can't put you in danger again. It's not your job. You're not licensed as a private investigator," I said.

"Well, I'm not investigating, am I?" she said.

I looked at her. "Well, I guess not."

"So where are we going?" she asked.

"Do you like to exercise?" I asked.

In spite of the little voice in the back of my head telling me not to, I made the call to the trainer. He seemed a little too excited about the prospect of training me. The guy made my skin crawl, but it was the price I'd have to pay if I wanted to catch the guy who had followed me.

Dorothy insisted that her beige linen pants and bright pink blouse were fine for going to the gym. I, however, had to change into workout clothes.

"I don't intend on breaking a sweat," she said with a clack of her knitting needles.

After hurrying into my apartment, I slipped into my black yoga pants—they were more slimming—and tank top. I rushed back outside and climbed behind the wheel, pointing the car in the direction of the gym. Much to my chagrin, the parking lot was full of cars. That would mean the place would be full of sweating bodies. I had my fingers crossed that there would be at least one more female on the premises.

When Dorothy and I stepped into the place, not one person looked up to notice us. They were all too busy watching their reflections in the wall-to-wall mirrors. My new trainer must have sensed the presence of someone without muscles because he glanced over and looked right at us.

When he saw Dorothy he frowned. I hadn't told him about the added bonus of my knitting needle-carrying assistant. He set his dumbbells down and walked over to us. He smiled and then looked from me to Dorothy.

"I didn't know you were bringing your grandmother," he said.

"You got a problem with that?" Dorothy asked.

He held his hands up in surrender. "No, no problem."

"Dorothy is my assistant," I said. "She wants to do a little exercise too."

"I'll just walk on the treadmill." She waved over her shoulder and marched toward the machine as if she'd been to this gym a million times before.

Heck, I wouldn't be surprised to find out that she had been to the gym many more times than I had.

"So what do you want to tone up first? Those flabby arms or your stomach? How about firming up that butt?" he asked looking me up and down.

I quirked a brow. "I'm not that flabby."

"Well, no, but everyone can tone up a little, right? That's why you called me, huh?"

"Um, yeah, sure, that's why I called you," I said.

I stretched my arms and legs, reaching down and touching my toes. I wanted to be ready to sprint if I had to chase someone. Oh, who was I kidding? I wanted to be ready to run from my crazy personal trainer.

This guy had had way too much caffeine because he started me off right away—lunges, chest presses, bicep curls, and triceps dips. I wouldn't be able to move tomorrow.

While I was doing a squat, I spotted the guy who had followed me. Now what would I do? I hadn't thought this plan through well. I straightened my legs until I was in a standing position again.

"I need a drink of water," I said without giving Erich the chance to say no.

I marched toward the front of the gym.

When I neared the treadmill, I called to Dorothy. "We have to go."

Dorothy was moving so slowly on the treadmill I wondered if the thing was even on.

"Had enough of the workout, huh?" she asked as if she'd been waiting for this moment since we arrived.

"The guy who followed us just walked out the front door. We have to follow him," I whispered.

That statement got Dorothy moving fast. She climbed down from the treadmill and rushed past, beating me to the door.

By the time we made it outside, the guy had jumped into his car. I snapped a couple of photos of him. It occurred to me that spying and following was good, but was I really doing all that I could to find out who these people really were? I knew I had to follow this guy, but that didn't mean I shouldn't find out all I could about the suspects whose names I already had. I needed to research any court filings against them and check their property records.

All of this might end up being fruitless, but I had to give it a try. Then I'd go back to the gym and ask everyone in the place if they recognized this guy. Now that I had his picture it would be easier to ask who he was. Those guys would probably sing like canaries for a few protein bars and shakes.

There was only one thing to do. I had to follow him. Dorothy and I jumped into my car and we peeled out of the parking lot. Confrontation probably wasn't the best idea, now that I thought about it. I didn't want to get myself into another iffy situation where bullets were whizzing past my head. Spying might give me more information without the risk of an altercation. If I did end up catching this guy, I'd immediately back off before a confrontation.

When I glanced in the rearview mirror, my trainer was standing outside the gym shaking his head. No doubt he figured I'd given up. Whatever. He deserved it for that comment about my butt.

We were headed down the street, and I knew this guy had no idea that we were following him. If he was clueless, then I was even worse because I had no idea what I was going to do if I found out

where he was going. Maybe his destination would give me answers. I'd find out the reason he'd followed me in the first place. Had he seen me at the gym? If so, why hadn't he confronted me?

"What are you going to say to this guy if you catch him?" Dorothy must have read my mind.

"Well, I don't know for sure. I should ask him why he's following me," I said.

"If he is some random stalker, then I wouldn't recommend that," Dorothy said.

"I'll take him down and make him cry," I said.

Dorothy rolled her eyes, seeing right through my fake tough-guy act.

Dorothy rattled her purse and pulled out a peppermint. She unwrapped it and stuck it up to my mouth. "Here, suck on this. It'll calm your nerves."

Those little peppermints were a cure-all as far as she was concerned. Instead of arguing with her about the fact that I really didn't want one, I just took it from her and popped it into my mouth. At least my breath would be minty fresh.

Chapter Twenty-Two

After many turns and almost losing the black car more than once, we followed it into an office building parking lot. I stayed at the back of the lot while the other car drove to the front row of parking spaces and pulled into a spot by the door.

I backed my car into a spot close to the exit in case I needed to make a fast getaway. I waited for what seemed like forever but the man didn't get out of his car. My heart thumped in my ears. I just knew that he was aware that I'd followed him here. Why else was he just sitting in his car?

"What do you think he's doing in there?" Dorothy asked.

"He's probably contemplating ways to kill me," I said.

"Don't worry, honey. If he comes at us, I'll poke his eyes out with my knitting needles," she said.

I stared at her for a moment. I didn't doubt her for two seconds. Dorothy would do it if she had to. She might look like a sweet little grandma, but I was sure if you messed with her she'd kick your ass. Finally, when I'd almost given up on him ever getting out of the car, he opened the door and climbed out from behind the wheel.

The man walked toward the entrance of the building, but as he neared the door, he paused. He looked to his left and then to his right. I knew he sensed us watching him. If he followed his

instincts and looked over his shoulder, he would probably spot four little eyes glaring at him from across the parking lot.

"Dorothy, if he looks back here we need to duck," I said.

"Don't you think that will be a little too conspicuous?" she asked.

She did have a point, but it was better than doing nothing. After several seconds of holding my breath, I watched as the man continued toward the door, opened it, and disappeared inside.

"What do we do now?" Dorothy asked.

"We wait," I said.

We settled in for the long haul—me with my binoculars and Dorothy with her knitting needles. I wasn't going to ask her not to do that anymore, because she was too set in her ways. Maybe she could knit me a binocular cozy or something.

The click-clack of Dorothy's needles was making me drowsy. I yawned and forced my eyelids open.

"How long has he been in there, anyway? An hour? Two hours?" I glanced down at my watch.

Okay, it had been only ten minutes. This was getting me nowhere. After another couple of minutes, another car pulled up. It parked right beside the car that we'd followed. This wouldn't have been a big deal but as we watched, two men got out, walked towards the building, then paused by the other car and peered in the windows.

After circling the car a couple times, they went into the building. There had to be a way for me to find out what was going on inside. Watching from afar while Dorothy knitted wasn't getting me anything, other than learning how to cast on.

Slipping up to the building and either listening in at the door or going inside was my only option. But did I really have the nerve to try something like that? I was about to find out. If they caught me I'd have to come up with a good lie as to why I was

there. Who was I kidding? Any excuse I gave they'd know was a lie right away.

"Dorothy, I'm not getting anywhere out here just watching them. I need to hear what they're saying," I said.

She quirked an eyebrow. "And how do you intend to do that?"

I glanced away so that she couldn't glare at me any longer. This was exactly like investigating with a grandmother except I didn't have a chocolate chip cookie in my hand right now.

"I'm going closer to the building to see if I can eavesdrop," I said.

"Have you lost your mind? What if they catch you?" she asked.

"I won't let that happen. Don't worry. You'll be my lookout, okay? If someone comes, just distract them," I said.

"How do I do that?" she asked.

"Honk the horn."

She released a deep sigh. "Well, I'll give it my best shot."

I got out of the car and tried to make my way toward the building while hiding behind cars. I tried to act as casual as possible under the circumstances. It was really tough to hide behind a palm tree.

Finally, I made it to the main door of the building. It was glass and the walls surrounding it were glass as well. I walked past a couple times, looking into the building. There was a lobby, but it was empty. On the left and right were closed doors. I wasn't sure which room the men were in, but the only way I'd find out was to go inside. There was no turning back now. Well, I guess if I'd wanted to be a chicken, I could have turned back, but I had to prove to myself that I could do this.

I opened the door and stepped into the lobby. Which door would I find them behind? Door number one, two, three . . . ? I moved from door to door, but heard nothing. When I reached the fourth door on the right, I heard voices, but I couldn't make out what was being said.

I may have been new at this, but I wasn't completely clueless. I'd brought my bag with me and had a few gadgets. After digging the equipment out of the bag, I placed it up to the wood and listened through the door with the contact surface microphone. Dorothy had suggested holding a glass to the door, but trust me, I'd tried that before with little result. This new gadget was much better.

With my ear pressed up to the device, I listened to their discussion. Now I needed to figure out if anything they said would offer me a clue. So far, they were discussing what they'd had for lunch. I was potentially risking my life for that?

"Do you have the information?" one of the men asked.

"You'll find all the details here," another man said.

"Sam Louis?" the man asked.

What? Why was he mentioning his name? What did he have to do with this? Had Sam Louis hired this guy? This had to be related to the other man who'd followed me. Were they all involved with Sam? My heart rate increased.

When the sound of moving chairs started, I almost threw the device across the room. I stuffed the equipment back into my bag and ran toward the door. With clumsy hands, I opened the door and bolted out of the office building. I ran so fast I could barely catch my breath. When I reached the car, I opened the door and jumped in.

"What did you find out? When I saw you running out the door, I thought I was going to have to use those knitting needles after all," Dorothy said.

"I need to talk with Sam Louis. He may have answers to the murders . . . or he may be the murderer," I said.

"Is that what you heard?" she asked.

I nodded. "Sort of. They mentioned his name."

I wondered if Allison had spoken with Sam since she'd been arrested. It was time to pay him a visit and get some answers. First thing in the morning, I was headed to his house.

But right now, I owed Dorothy a Bunco game. At least this time it wouldn't be next door to Jake's house. I had found the game and being surrounded by the women to be oddly relaxing.

"Where's the game tonight? It's at another member's house, right?" I asked.

As much as I didn't want to admit it, I was totally getting into this Bunco stuff. It was a little addictive. It required about as much skill as coloring with crayons, but it was strangely fun. Maybe I just enjoyed the company. The women had a lot of fun.

"Oh, it's at Mary's place again. Jeanine is having her bathroom remodeled so Mary agreed to host the party again," Dorothy said.

"No way. I can't go tonight," I shook my head. "I'll take you to your car so that you can drive there."

"Is this all because you're afraid to run into that detective? Why are you fighting it? Just go with the flow. If it's meant to be, then it'll be. Don't you date?" She scowled.

"Yes, I date when I have time," I said.

She looked at me suspiciously. "When's the last time you had a date?"

"Well, today makes two weeks since I stopped worrying about it," I said.

She snorted. "You really should get out more."

"I have a very full social life," I said.

"You're young, and so far all I can see is you're working, working, working," she said.

"It takes a while for a business to get started and from what Uncle Griffin left me there is a lot of work to be done. Anyway, there will be time for fun when I retire." I winked.

"If you don't slow down and smell the ocean breeze, life will pass you by," Dorothy said.

When we pulled up to the condo, I circled around until I found an empty space. I didn't want to make the same mistake and take

Jake's parking place again. After finding a spot that I thought was safe, I hurried out of the car and toward the building. I didn't bother to look over at his parking space.

I'd almost made it to the condo door when the sound of a car pulling up behind us caught my attention. In spite of myself, I had to turn around and look. When I saw Jake's smiling face, I wanted to run away. Dorothy grabbed my arm and stopped my escape. Jake looked handsome—as usual—as he got out of his car.

"Wow, am I missing Bunco night again?" he asked with a smile.

Yes, and if I could get Dorothy to release her hold on my arm, I'd miss it too.

"I have a great idea. Why don't you join us tonight?" Dorothy asked. "We have food." She wiggled her eyebrows.

There was no way he would agree to it, right? "I'm sure he has a lot of police stuff to do," I said.

"As a matter of fact, I'm free. I'd love to go," he said with a smile.

When we entered the condo, the room fell silent, but all eyes were on Jake. Of course, he was the only man in the room.

"Ladies, this is Jake Jackson. He's a detective with the Miami Police." Dorothy held on to Jake's arm.

The entire room sighed with delight.

"Nice to meet you, Jake," the women said in unison.

"What about me, Dorothy?" I poked her in the arm.

"Oh yeah, you all remember Maggie Thomas from last time." Dorothy guided Jake away, leaving me standing there.

The women didn't offer a cheery greeting to me. Instead, their eyes followed Jake across the room.

"The ladies will be really excited about having a handsome man here tonight," Dorothy said with a smile.

Jake just smiled. He was probably enjoying the attention.

"Maggie, you sit beside your handsome date," Mary said with a smile.

"He's not my date," I said as I looked at Mary. I ignored Jake's stare. "He's not my date," I said as I looked at the other women's smiling faces.

Jake winked at me, which made the situation even worse.

It was hard to concentrate with Jake sitting beside me, especially when his manly scent kept tickling my nostrils. Too bad I didn't have an air neutralizer to block out the smell.

"You're pretty good at this. Are you sure you haven't played before?" I asked.

"Nope, this is my first time." He stared at me with a devilish smile.

"You know if you win the ladies will be upset," I said.

"Oh, we don't care. He can win if he wants to," Mary said, wiggling her eyebrows.

I rolled my eyes. It was really sweet that he'd taken the time to play with the women. And he seemed to genuinely enjoy it, too.

Just as the game was over, and yes, Jake had won, a car alarm sounded in the parking lot. It was blazingly loud. Who had such an annoying car alarm? While Jake collected his gift of lace-trimmed hand towels, I stepped over to the door and peered out, hoping to find the offending car. I scanned the lot and my eyes fell on my car.

"Hey, that's my car," I announced.

The lights were flashing and the screeching noise penetrated the air. What had set it off? Had someone tried to steal my car? That was the last thing I needed.

The woman shuffled as fast as they could over to the windows. They hadn't seen this much action since ... well, since Jake had shown up to play Bunco with them. Dorothy inched her way in beside me.

"What happened?" she asked breathlessly.

"Someone or something set off my car alarm," I said.

"Why is it so loud?" she asked covering her ears.

Working his way through the maze of women, Jake came over and stood beside us. "What happened?" he asked in a calm voice.

"My alarm was set off," I said.

"Alarms go off all the time. It was probably just a vibration in the ground. Maybe from another car driving by. Your alarm is probably super sensitive."

"It's never gone off before." I frowned.

"Well, there's a first for everything," he said.

"Yeah, well, I wonder if it's going off because of that guy who is messing around it?" a woman asked as she pointed out the window.

I followed her pointing finger and saw a man around my car. This guy had something in common with the other one who had been following me: big muscles. He looked just like the other gym rats.

Jake didn't say a word as he took off out the door after the perp. I ran outside after him. I heard the stampede of women following behind us. Well, a slow stampede. Jake weaved through cars and I ran as hard as I could to keep up with his pace. Unfortunately his legs were much longer than mine and could cover more distance a lot faster. When I got my hands on this guy, I was going to clobber him. What did he think he was doing messing around my car? Maybe I could finally get an answer as to why he was following me.

Just as Jake approached the car, another car pulled up nearby. It looked awfully familiar.

"That's the car that has been following me," I said.

Jake glanced at me with a look of confusion. Yeah, I hadn't told him about the multiple cars following me. Telling him might have hampered my investigation. Maybe that was a stupid move on my part, but it was what I'd decided to do nonetheless.

I never claimed to be perfect or have all the right answers. The man darted to his left and ran for the waiting car. The car door opened and he jumped in. The car sped away, its tires screeching

as it made a turn around the building. I looked on in shock. When I looked over my shoulder, all the women were standing behind us, staring with their mouths open.

Jake ran for his car. I barely had time to register what he was doing before he had jumped in, cranked the ignition, and taken off after the car. I hoped he found the men, but I wasn't optimistic. They had a knack for getting away. I watched as Jake sped out of the parking lot in pursuit of the car.

"Well, at least we got to finish the game before this happened," one of the women said from over my shoulder.

Dorothy stood beside me. "That looked like one of the muscle men."

I nodded and ran my hand through my hair. "Yes, and it was the same car. Now we have a gang of bodybuilders after us."

Mary was standing to the side with a distressed look on her face.

"I'm sorry that this happened, Mary," I said.

She nodded. "That's okay."

She spoke the words, but I knew she still had reservations about what had happened. There was no way I was coming back for another Bunco game. Not that they would ever invite me again, but I wouldn't put these women in harm's way. I didn't want Dorothy to be involved either, although I doubted I'd be able to convince her to stay out of it.

When I glanced back at Dorothy, she had a frown on her face and was staring at my car.

"There's something on the window," she said.

I followed her stare and spotted the little piece of paper secured to the windshield of my car. Dorothy immediately took off toward my car and I followed in pursuit. I whizzed around her and grabbed the note from under the windshield wiper. I unfolded it as Dorothy watched from over my shoulder.

You're next was scribbled in sloppy writing.

"How utterly unoriginal, yet frightening at the same time," I said.

"This has gone too far," Dorothy fumed. "What would their mothers think?" She scowled. "They should be ashamed of their behavior."

"Yes, they should be, but I highly doubt that they are," I said.

As Dorothy and I debated the note, Jake drove back from around the building and pulled up beside my car. He jumped out and hurried over to us.

"Did you find them?" I asked hopefully.

He frowned and shook his head. "No, they got away. I wasn't able to find them, but I do have police looking for the car. Don't worry, though, I won't stop until I find out who they are."

I had no doubt that he meant what he said. There was a look of determination in his eyes that I'd never seen before.

"There's more," Dorothy said.

She wasn't going to let me keep the note from Jake. What could he do? Test it for fingerprints? Okay, so he actually *could* test it for fingerprints, but that was neither here nor there.

Jake frowned. "What else?"

"They left a note. Show him, Maggie." Dorothy poked me in the side.

I scowled at her then turned to meet Jake's stare.

"May I see the note?" he asked in a calm tone.

I stared at him for a beat, then finally handed over the note. "There's not much to it. It's kind of lame, actually. I mean, who leaves notes like that? It's so utterly cheesy it's comical."

He met my gaze. "Do you see me laughing?"

"Yeah, do you see him laughing?" Dorothy said.

Whose side was she on, anyway?

"I'm not laughing, either," she added.

Okay, so neither of them was amused by the note.

"Look, I don't like that they left it either, but I'm sure it's all talk. Someone is just trying to scare me, but it's not going to work," I said.

"Maybe it should work," Dorothy said under her breath.

"Who do you think left this note for you?" Jake asked.

I shrugged. "My guess is they have something to do with the murder of Arthur Abbott. Maybe I'm a little too close to finding out who did it. Are you going to believe me now that Allison didn't murder her husband?" I asked.

"Why didn't you tell me this car had been following you?" Jake asked.

"I was handling it," I said with a smirk.

The police arrived within a couple minutes and began searching in and around my car. I couldn't say that I liked them poking through my stuff. They looked at me suspiciously when they saw all the surveillance gear.

"Let me drive you home," Jake said as he watched me with his piercing eyes.

"I'm not leaving my car here," I said, looking at him like he'd lost his mind.

He blew out a deep breath and then said, "Okay, well let me follow you home."

Yeah, he'd like that, wouldn't he?

"Private eyes don't have escorts home. I'm tough. I can handle it," I said with determination in my voice.

I wouldn't let him think I was a damsel in distress. I was a professional and I wanted him to treat me as such.

The women had gone back into the condo. The police still lingered around. I was just thankful that Jake hadn't thought to have my car towed as evidence. He'd have had even more of an excuse to drive me home then.

I climbed behind the wheel and closed the door. Jake leaned down and stared at me.

"What?" I asked.

"You'll tell me if anything else like this happens?" he asked.

I crossed my fingers so that he couldn't see them. "Of course I will." I smiled.

"Why don't I believe you?" he asked as he looked at me suspiciously.

I shrugged. "I guess you have trust issues."

He smiled.

Chapter Twenty-Three

While on my way home that night, the creepy sensation of someone following me had overcome me. I'd been careful and not taken my usual route home. I'd even watched in the rearview mirror and hadn't seen a car following me, or so I'd thought. Still, that feeling stuck with me.

I'd finally found a spot on the street and jumped out, looking around in the dark night. Palm fronds brushed against tree trunks and a ruffling of bushes nearby made me jump. I hurried up to my apartment, glancing over my shoulder multiple times. I was just being paranoid. But I pulled my gun out of its holster just so I'd be prepared if anyone showed up and tried to cause me a problem.

Once inside my apartment, I secured the door and peeked out the window. I scanned the area. When I looked to my right, I spotted movement around the palm trees. Someone stepped out of the shadows and walked away from the apartment.

So someone had been watching me after all. The person wasn't as muscular as the bodybuilders, so I knew it wasn't one of them. Unfortunately, it was dark and I couldn't make out any features—only that it was a man. I decided to sleep with my weapon by the bed. Things were getting too scary. What would my father have done in this situation?

I kicked off my shoes and cranked up the AC. I considered myself lucky that the place had air conditioning—even if it didn't work well. It made a groaning noise all night long, as if it just wanted me to put it out of its misery, but I'd gotten used to the noise after a few days and now it was almost soothing in a weird way. I collapsed onto the bed and the next thing I knew, morning broke across my face.

When I stepped into my office, Dorothy was waiting for me by the door. I clutched my chest. "What are you trying to do? Scare the hell out of me?"

"I saw you coming across the parking lot." She grabbed my arm. "Come on. We have a mission and it involves going to that gym and finding those men."

How could I say no to that?

At least we hadn't been followed on our way to the gym. Well, I was pretty sure no one had followed us. I glanced around the parking lot as I hurried across, but so far it seemed safe. Though an abundance of people working out filled the room, there was no sign of the men when I stepped inside.

"There you are." Erich pointed at me as I made my way across the gym. "I figured you'd never come back again. Was my workout too much for you?" he asked with a creepy smile.

"Yeah. I had a leg cramp," I said, pointing toward my leg.

"You've just got to work through it," he said, while looking me up and down.

"I'll keep that in mind. Look, I'm not here to talk about working out," I said, while glancing around to see who might be watching us.

His face lit up and I instantly knew that this guy thought he was getting laid. He probably thought I was going to slip into the locker room with him and do it right there. He stepped closer and I backed up a couple steps.

I'd printed off one of the pictures I'd taken of the goon who'd been following me.

I pulled the photo from my pocket. "Do you recognize this guy?"

He frowned and took the photo from my outstretched hand. His brows drew together in concentration as he studied the photo. Finally, he looked up at me. His expression had changed. It was no longer at ease.

He shook his head. "I've never seen him."

I studied Erich's face. I knew he wasn't being truthful with me, but what could I do? I couldn't force him to tell me the truth.

I gave him the widest, sweetest smile. "Are you sure you've never seen him?"

He frowned and shook his head frantically. "Nope."

Okay, I hadn't really expected him to fall for the fake smile.

"I have another client. I have to go." He turned and hurried away, disappearing into the men's locker room.

"Coward," I called out across the gym.

No one even looked up at my comment. They were still too consumed by their pecs.

"Having problems?" a male voice asked from over my shoulder.

I spun around to find the guy who had landed face first off the treadmill.

"Yeah, you could say that," I said around a sigh.

"That guy isn't much of a personal trainer, huh?" he asked with a slight smile.

I shook my head. "No, not really." With the guy still staring at me, I figured it wouldn't hurt to ask if he'd seen my suspect. "Have you seen this guy?"

He took the photo from my hand, but his expression didn't sink the way that my trainer's had.

"Yeah, he's in here all the time. Why are you looking for him?" He met my gaze.

"It's a private matter," I said.

He shook his head. "Fair enough."

"So I see you didn't have any lasting damage from the other day." I pointed at his legs.

He chuckled. "That was not one of my finer moments."

If he'd seen this guy, then I had to push for more details.

"Do you happen to know this man's name?" I asked innocently.

He stared at me for a moment. "You have his picture, but you don't know his name?"

I looked around the room to see who might be listening to our conversation. Then I remembered where we were and I knew that no one would bother to listen in.

But I lowered my voice just in case. "Okay, fine. I'm a private investigator and I've been hired to find him."

That wasn't entirely a lie. I was a private eye, but I didn't want him to know that this guy had been stalking me. But now I had turned the tables and was stalking him.

His eyebrows rose. "Interesting. A private investigator. That's cool. His name is Chuck, but I don't know the last name. Sorry."

I stuffed the picture back in my pocket. "Thanks. That helps a lot."

"No problem," he said as he ran his hand through his hair. "My name's Keith Manchester."

"Maggie Thomas," I said with a smile. "Nice to meet you."

"The pleasure is all mine," he said with a smile.

Keith had only offered the man's first name, but it was definitely better than nothing. I needed to act on this newly discovered information right away.

"Well, thanks for the information and it was really nice talking with you, but I have to go now," I said as I motioned toward the door.

As I walked away, he asked, "Will I see you again?"

I looked back and smiled. "Maybe."

Now I had his first name, but what would I do with that? As I walked by the front desk on my way toward the gym's door, an idea popped into my head. Adrenaline raced through my body at the thought. I looked around to see if anyone was watching me. Keith had climbed back on the treadmill, so unless he fell off again, I didn't think he'd notice what I was about to do.

The gym's computer was behind the counter. The members scanned their cards when they walked in. I had just a temporary guest pass. All member information must be stored in that computer.

Giving one last glance around the room, I hurried behind the desk. The employee who was supposed to be manning the desk was asleep on the floor in the office. I heard his snoring and peeked in. He was practically asking for me to steal the information. I leaned over the keyboard and typed the first name into the search box. I was no expert at computers, so I prayed that I didn't mess the whole thing up. I typed in the name Chuck. Unfortunately, Chuck was a common name and about twenty Chucks popped up. Maybe Chuck was short for Charles? I'd have to check that name too. How would I know which one was my stalker? There had to be a way to narrow it down. I was running out of time. Soon someone would notice that I wasn't supposed to be behind this desk.

Just then the main door opened and a member walked through it. I froze, unable to take my eyes off this bulky man. Would he say something? Ask me what the hell I was doing back there?

He nodded and said, "What's up?"

Before he even gave me a chance to respond, he walked on through to the main area of the gym. Whew. He must have thought I worked there. I focused my attention on the screen again and scanned the options. That was when I hit pay dirt. There was an option to display the gym members' photos. I glanced over my shoulder and clicked the mouse, praying that I wouldn't be caught red-handed.

Tiny photos appeared next to each name. The pictures were small, but I recognized my guy's face right away and clicked to enlarge it. A larger image of his face appeared along with his last name and address. I grabbed the pen and pad of paper next to the computer and scribbled down the details, then rushed from around the desk. It was kind of disturbing to know just how easily I'd discovered this man's address.

When I made it to the door, I glanced back. That was when I noticed Keith watching me. He frowned and climbed off the treadmill. I turned around and rushed out the door, not giving him a chance to ask what I'd been doing. He was awfully nosy. Why was he so interested in what I was doing?

I hurried across the parking lot back to the car.

As I jumped in breathlessly, Dorothy asked, "Did you find him?"

"Not exactly, but I found his home address." I waved the paper in the air.

"What are you going to do with that?" She looked at me with wide eyes.

"Well, I figured I'd send him a birthday card. What do you think? We're going to his house." I cranked the engine.

She waved her finger in my direction. "Don't you be sassy with me, young lady."

I sighed as I shoved the gearshift into reverse. "Sorry."

She shook her head. "I can't allow you to go to his home. It's just too dangerous."

She couldn't allow me? There wasn't much she could do to convince me not to go.

I steered the car out onto the street. "Now Dorothy, you already know that I'm not going to listen to you and will immediately drive straight to his house."

"You are too stubborn for your own good," she said around a sigh.

Within a few minutes, we pulled up to the apartment building. I prayed that my GPS had taken me to the right place. It was a stucco building that contained six different apartments.

"His apartment is number six. I'm going to knock on his door and see if he's home," I said as I opened my door.

"I want no part of this," she said, taking her needles out of her purse.

She wouldn't even look up at me. What a way to make a girl feel guilty.

"Oh, Dorothy, don't be mad at me," I pleaded as I climbed out of the car.

She scowled and shook her head, but said nothing in return. I didn't have time to discuss it right now. She'd get over it. This was part of my job.

Palm trees lined the street and shrubs edged the sidewalk. I stepped up onto the stoop and turned around to look at Dorothy as she sat in the car. She was watching me until she realized that I had turned around, and then she looked down and feverishly went back to her knitting.

I sucked in a deep breath and opened the door leading inside the building. Once in the little hallway, I marched over to the door marked number six. For a moment I thought about turning around and making my way back to the car before he caught me standing at his front door, but then I realized this was something that I had to do.

With my fist, I knocked on the door loudly. I glanced down and noticed a doorbell so I pushed it. Nothing happened, so I knocked again. The hallway was well lit with a line of mailboxes on the opposite wall. I noticed his last name marked on the number six, so that reaffirmed that I had the right place.

What was taking this guy so long? I'd thought I'd heard movement from the other side of the door. Maybe he'd seen me and decided not to answer.

I pounded on the door again, but this time it opened with the force of my fist. I stepped back and looked around.

"Hello, is anyone home?" I called out.

No one answered. Was this guy just playing games with me? I pushed the door open wider with my foot and called out again. Still no one answered and I didn't hear any more sounds from the other side. Dorothy would have a fit when she found out what I was about to do, but it had to be done. I eased inside the door, stopping at the threshold.

"Is anyone home?" I asked again.

The room was sparsely decorated, with a blue sofa on the wall closest to me and a large TV across from it. A glass coffee table sat in the middle of the room. Clothes were strewn across the sofa and empty food containers littered the table. It looked like he was a huge Taco Bell fan.

I had no idea—now that I was in the apartment—what I was going to do. Why had I come inside? I guess the fact that the door had been open made me wonder if I'd step inside and find another dead man. I prayed that wasn't the case this time. Two bodies were enough for me.

I peeked down the hallway into the bedroom, but didn't see anyone. I started to get the creeps now, so I figured I needed to get out of there fast. As I turned around, I noticed a piece of paper on the kitchen table. I stepped closer and picked up the paper. The only thing written on the page was an address, but I recognized it right away. It was the address for the law firm. This was the clue that I needed. It linked him to the murders in some way, but how exactly? I clasped the page in my hand.

When I turned around to leave, I jumped and clutched my chest. The piece of paper flew out of my hand. Dorothy was standing beside me.

"You scared the hell out of me," I said, trying to catch my breath.

She pounded me on the back to help me breathe normally as if I was choking.

"What are you doing here?" I asked.

"Well, I came to save your butt," she said as she looked around the messy apartment.

"What makes you think I needed saving?" I asked, picking the paper up from the floor.

"Just a hunch," she said sarcastically.

"Come on. Let's get out of here before we get caught. I don't know how I'd explain the fact that we're standing in this man's house," I said as I headed toward the door.

As we made it to the door, a sound came from behind me. When I looked over my shoulder, I saw a guy standing in the hallway with a towel draped around his waist. He'd been in the shower, of course. Why hadn't I realized that water had been running? Darn.

"What the hell are you doing in here?" he yelled.

The muscle man ran toward us, but with his movement, the towel fell to the floor.

"Whoa," Dorothy said as she glanced back.

How had I ended up in a naked man's apartment? Oh yeah—I'd walked right in like a fool. He didn't seem to mind that he was now fully exposed. His bottom half wasn't nearly as large as the top half. As I fumbled with the doorknob, trying to get it open, he lunged at me. Thank goodness his hand didn't make contact with me.

The guy ran after us as we spilled out into the hallway. I should have confronted him, considering he had been following me around, but he seemed awfully angry at the moment and I didn't have my gun or stun gun on me. What if he really wanted to kill us? I didn't want to endanger Dorothy's life any more than I already had. By the shade of red covering his face, I figured he'd snap me in two if he got his hands on me. With any luck, he wouldn't get the opportunity.

When I finally got the main door open, I pushed Dorothy out first and then slipped out of the apartment building right behind her. The distance from the building to my car seemed a lot longer now that our lives were in danger. I glanced over at Dorothy to make sure she was all right, but she was already ahead of me. How had she run so quickly? I pushed the key fob, unlocking the doors, and Dorothy scurried inside. I yanked the driver's side open and jumped in, locking the doors behind us. The man was still running toward us, and still in his birthday suit. The muscles must have slowed him down because two out-of-shape women had just outrun him. I cranked the car and managed to pull out, leaving the guy standing in the middle of the parking lot.

"Well, that was a close call," Dorothy said, blowing a few loose strands of hair out of her eyes.

"I think I really pissed him off," I said.

"You'd be angry too if your manly parts shrank in the shower," Dorothy quipped.

Chapter Twenty-Four

The next day, before going into the office, I headed to Sam Louis's address. I called Dorothy and told her I'd be late, but I didn't explain where I was headed. She thought I was going shopping for more detective supplies. I'd told a little fib, but it was for her own good.

When I pulled up to the large house, a car was pulling out of the driveway. Sam Louis was at the wheel. If he wanted out of the driveway, he'd have to go through me first. I pulled my car up across the driveway and blocked him from pulling out. He wasn't going anywhere until I asked him a few questions.

When I stepped out of my car, he jumped out of his.

"Hey, you need to get out of the way," he yelled, gesturing for me to move.

His face turned red.

"Mr. Louis, I need to ask you a few questions regarding the death of your law firm partner," I said, getting right to the point.

"Why are you here?" he asked with a frown.

If he had someone following me, then he knew very well who I was.

"My name is Maggie Thomas. I'm a private investigator hired by Arthur Abbott's wife," I said with determination in my voice.

The red immediately vanished from his face.

"She hired you?" he asked.

He had to have known that she hired me. He was just playing dumb. I walked closer.

"Yes, she did. I just have a few quick questions. You don't mind answering my questions, do you?" I asked, staring him right in the eyes.

Had he even been to see the woman he claimed to be so in love with? He should be trying desperately to get her out of jail. But maybe he wanted her to stay there. Maybe he'd used her so that he'd have her to take the rap for the murder that he'd committed. But why would he kill Arthur? What was his motive? Something told me that he wouldn't be forthcoming with me.

"Sure, I guess can answer your questions," he said as he looked at his watch.

"Do you know who killed Arthur Abbott?" I asked.

It was worth a shot just to see what his reaction would be.

His eyes widened. "Don't you think if I knew who did this that I'd tell the police?"

"So you don't believe that Allison killed her husband?" I asked pointedly.

His expression saddened. "No, I don't think she did it."

"Have you been to see her since she's been in jail?" I asked, as I examined his expression for a clue of the truth.

"She doesn't want to see me anymore," he said, looking away.

"Why do you say that?" I asked.

"She told me so on the day of his murder. She broke things off," he said, clearly angered by having to tell me something so personal. "She broke off our relationship. I don't think she wants me to visit her."

So that was why she'd taken the walk on the beach? To think things through? Plus, Allison had gone to the condo. Obviously to

tell her husband that she'd stopped seeing Sam. But why hadn't she shared this pertinent information with me?

I nodded, but decided to switch gears. "Do you know of anyone who would have a reason to kill him?"

He looked away, avoiding my gaze, then said, "No, I don't know of anyone."

"Just one more thing," I said.

"Yes?" he asked.

"Did you have someone follow me?" I asked.

"I'm finished with this conversation," he said.

I released a deep breath. "Well, you'll call me if you think of anything, right?"

He looked me in the eye and nodded. "Now if you'll excuse me, I need to get going. I'm late for a deposition." He gestured toward his car.

I stared for a breath, then nodded. "Yeah, okay. Thanks for talking to me."

That had yielded little information, but Sam Louis hadn't seemed completely forthcoming when I asked if he knew of anyone who'd wanted to kill Arthur or if someone had followed me. Was he keeping something from me?

I needed to head by the gym and look for the goons who had left the note on my car. I wasn't afraid to confront them—maybe I should have been, but I wasn't. So what if the guy had chased me out of his apartment? He couldn't do anything to me in a public place, right? But before I did that, there was one other thing that I'd do.

Now that Sam was gone, it wouldn't hurt to look around a little bit, right? In his haste to get away from me, he'd left his garage door open. I glanced around the quiet neighborhood. In the distance a man walked his little white dog, but he was headed in the opposite direction and I didn't think he'd noticed me. A woman a few houses down backed out of her driveway in her SUV. She glanced

in my direction, but we didn't make eye contact, so I wasn't sure if she'd seen me.

I likely wouldn't find anything, but it was my job to snoop. How would I ever find answers if I didn't occasionally stick my nose where it didn't belong? From where I stood, the only items I saw in the garage were a lawnmower and a bicycle, but it was worth a look nonetheless. Since there were no other cars in the garage, I figured no one was home. At least I prayed no one was home. What if someone was in there, though? They'd wonder what I was doing snooping around their house. They'd probably think I was a burglar.

I locked my car door and walked up the long driveway toward the house. A bird flew from the top of one of the shrubs and I jumped, stopping to look around. The neighborhood was still eerily quiet. I wasn't used to such silence—no cars or honking horns. When I reached the open garage door, I paused and glanced back one last time. I inched into the space and looked around. The place was immaculate. Every item had a designated spot. Lawn care equipment on the left and racks with broom, shears, and other items hanging on the wall. A bicycle hung on the right-hand wall and a few storage bins were stacked underneath it on the floor. As much as I wanted to snoop, I knew that there was no reason for me to look inside the bins. There was a door on the wall in front of me that led into the house. That door was probably locked. I'd gotten lucky that he'd left the garage door open. Besides, what would I do even if it was unlocked?

A muffled sound floated through the air. What was the noise? I climbed the two small steps and pressed my ear against the door. The sound came again. But this time I knew it was someone calling out. They were asking for help. Over and over they said the word *help*. But it was just a muffled voice, barely audible. If only I could get in to help this person.

I twisted the doorknob, but just as I'd suspected, the door was locked. I had to get in to help this person. Why had he left

someone who was obviously in distress? I rattled the door again and banged on it.

"Is anyone in there? Are you okay?" I yelled.

No one answered and the muffled voice calling out for help had stopped too. I had no choice but to get into the house. There wasn't time to call the police. I ran out onto the driveway and looked around for help, but the neighborhood was dead quiet; no one was outside their homes. I thought maybe a neighbor would have a key to the house. I'd have to figure out another way in.

I turned to my left and headed down the pathway toward the front door. The sprinklers had turned on, making the path wet, so I had to watch my footing. If I landed on my butt I wouldn't be of much help to the person inside who needed me. I ran up the front steps and twisted the front doorknob. Of course this door wouldn't open either, but it had been worth a shot. Sometimes people hid keys by the front door, so I looked around for a hiding spot. There were no fake rocks around and I checked under the mat but found nothing. I was running out of options. I'd have to put my feelings aside and call the police, much as I didn't want them involved. They would only want to know what I had been doing snooping around this house in the first place. Jake would definitely find out.

I decided to try a back door. As I sprinted across the lawn and around the house, I attempted to dodge the sprinklers. I slipped and almost lost my footing, but managed to remain upright. The pool at the back of the house was surrounded by a black gated fence. If that thing was locked then I'd have to climb the fence and I hadn't done that sort of thing in ages, probably not since I was seven years old and had climbed the tree in the front yard and then fibbed to my mother about it.

When I reached the gate, I moved the lever, but just as I'd feared, the gate was locked. I'd have to climb over the thing. I hoisted myself up and attempted to swing my leg over. After a

couple of grunts I got one leg over, but my shorts were caught on one of the posts. Now I was straddling this gate with my shorts attached. How would I explain myself to Jake when he saw me dangling on their gate?

I frantically pulled at my shorts; a loud ripping noise rang out. I was afraid to find out what damage I'd done to the shorts. I should have just swallowed my pride and called the police in the first place. Now that the fabric was loose I slipped my other leg over and rushed across the patio, careful to avoid the pool area. My clumsiness would probably kick in and I'd end up taking a little dip in the sparkling water.

I finally made it to the patio door, not bothering to peek in before trying the latch. It was probably locked. I mean, who would leave their door unlocked? But the door opened when I twisted the knob. My heart rate increased. Was I really going into this man's home? That was when I heard the muffled call for help again and I knew I had to save this person. If the door was open then it wasn't breaking and entering, right? Yeah, tell that to the judge.

With the door now open, I slipped into the house. The door led into the hearth room, which was connected to the kitchen. The ceilings were tall with beams and the kitchen had stainless steel appliances with granite and was bigger than ten of my apartments. The little voice was quiet. Had the person heard me enter the house?

"Hello?" I called out. "Is anyone home?"

"Help," the weak voice called out.

I made my way through the kitchen and into a long hallway. The blinds were drawn throughout the house so the space was dimly lit. The voice sounded again and I was sure it was coming from the room at the end of the hallway.

When I reached the door, I paused before entering, wondering if I was doing the right thing by being here. What if the killer was waiting for me? But why would the killer ask for help? Unless to lure me to my death. I pushed those thoughts out of my head and

opened the door. I had no idea what to expect, but the room was empty. The voice called out again.

I turned around to see if it came from behind me, but no one was there. That was when I saw the bird in its cage. It called out for help.

"Are you kidding me?" I said. "It was you?"

Who had taught him to say 'help'? Now I was standing in this man's house and I started to panic. There was no way to explain this away.

"You scared me." I waved my finger in the bird's direction. He didn't seem affected by what had happened.

I backed out of the room in a hurry and headed down the hallway. I had to get the hell out of there before I was caught. I rushed through the kitchen again, but stopped in my tracks when I saw pictures on the counter. I couldn't help but notice who was in the pictures. It was Arthur Abbott and a woman who wasn't his wife. She looked familiar and within seconds I knew where I recognized her from: she was Matt Cooper's wife. I'd seen her picture on his desk.

The photos showed them kissing and in a couple more comprising positions. I picked them up for a closer look, but I didn't need to see more; so I placed them back on the counter where I'd found them. What was going on in that law firm anyway?

As I placed the photos back on the counter, a business card fell to the floor. I reached down and picked it up. Two words under the person's name popped out at me. The card was for a private investigator? So Sam had used another private eye to snap these photos. I was a little disappointed that he hadn't hired me, but I couldn't get all the jobs in that law firm. I recognized the name on the front, but where had I seen the name before? It only took a couple seconds before it hit me: it was the guy from the gym. The klutz who couldn't stay on the treadmill without falling on his face. This made me furious. Why hadn't he told me who he was

when I told him I was a private investigator? What was he up to, anyway?

I'd almost made it to the back door when I heard a door open. My stomach dropped. What the heck would I do now? I was going to be caught. Where would I go now? How would I explain why I was in this house? I ran through a few ideas in my mind, but nothing sounded believable.

Footsteps were coming down the hall, so I knew I had to get out of there. I looked around the room for a hiding place. There was a sofa in the hearth room. I could hide behind it, but that wasn't the ideal location. Someone could come and have a seat and I'd be busted right away. That was when I spotted a door on the right. I opened it and realized it was a small closet. I stepped in and closed the door, praying that it wouldn't lock behind me or that the person wouldn't open it. I heard footsteps walking around the room. I held my breath and tried not to make a sound.

Was it Sam Louis? What was he doing back? Had he forgotten something? Maybe he'd forgotten to take the pictures with him. Why did he have photos of Arthur and Matt Cooper's wife? I'd have to find out answers about their affair.

I couldn't believe that I was hiding in that man's closet. The footsteps came closer and I thought for sure I would be caught at any moment. That was when I remembered that I'd left the back door open when I came in. The footsteps passed the closet. The back door that I'd left open was shut and I heard the lock click. The footsteps walked past again and I held my breath again. The person paused and I knew they were close to the door. My heart thumped wildly in my chest. I knew that they sensed my presence.

I couldn't stay in this tiny space for much longer. I was beginning to become claustrophobic. I hadn't known that I was claustrophobic until now. And I practically lived in a closet. Finally the footsteps moved again and went farther away. Then the front door clicked again and I prayed that he'd truly left the house.

I eased the closet door open and let out a deep breath. I peeked out and didn't see anyone, so I ran over to the back door and unlocked it. This guy would think that his place was haunted when he came home and the back door was unlocked again. I ran through the yard and climbed over the gate again. Thank goodness my shorts didn't get caught this time. I peeked around the side of the house. Wouldn't Sam have seen my car still parked on his street? That had to have made him suspicious.

When I made it to my car, I let out a huge sigh of relief and made it out of the subdivision before I got myself into any more trouble. All this over a bird. Now it was time to find out how long Arthur and Matt's wife had been having an affair. Wait until Dorothy found out about this.

Chapter Twenty-Five

After I felt I was a safe distance from the house, I pulled over so that I could dial the number on the card. Still angry, I punched the private investigator's number onto my screen and waited for it to ring. It rang countless times, but no one answered. Instead, the call went to his voice mail.

As much as I wanted to leave a sarcastic message, I decided it was best to keep my remarks to myself for the moment, so I just hung up. I pulled back onto the street and headed toward my house. I replayed the scene when I'd met Keith at the gym in my mind. He'd had plenty of opportunities to tell me who he was.

That was when an idea hit me. I steered my car over to the side of the road and pulled out the business card again. His address wasn't far away, so I decided to pay him a visit. Just as I was about to pull away from the curb, however, my phone beeped, letting me know I had a text message. I picked up the phone and peered at the screen. I had no idea Dorothy knew how to text. She wanted me to pick her up. Apparently, she was bored of knitting. I had created a private detecting monster.

Driving as fast as the speed limit would allow, I wheeled into the parking lot of my office. Dorothy was waiting outside the front door with her giant pocketbook draped across her arm.

She jumped in. "I thought you never would get here. Where are we headed this time?"

"It's good to see you too, Dorothy."

She whipped out a pair of binoculars. "I got my own pair," she said displaying a proud smile.

I bit back a laugh. "We're headed to the competition's place. Apparently there's been another private eye on the case and I never even knew it."

"Who?" she asked with her mouth draped open.

"It was that klutz from the gym who fell off the treadmill." I shook my head at the thought.

"I knew there was something wrong with that guy," she said.

If she'd known that much, why hadn't she told me earlier? I pulled up to the building and assessed the place to see if it was nicer than mine. Hey, he was the competition and I needed to see what I was up against. The building wasn't huge, but it was bigger and newer than my office. It had pretty landscaping and a large parking lot, but I had a view of the beach—albeit a small view, but it was still a view.

Dorothy hopped out of the car. "We'll see what this guy has to say for himself."

Dorothy had that giant bag draped across her arm and a look of determination in her eyes. He wouldn't know what hit him when she got done with him.

When I stepped into the office, a woman behind a desk greeted me. She was probably my age and had long dark hair and pretty brown eyes. She smiled widely as we walked toward her. On the right was a seating area with big leather chairs and even a TV in the corner. He must have a lot of business to afford something that nice.

"May I help you?" she asked cheerily.

"I'm here to see Keith Manchester."

"Sure. May I tell him who's here to see him?" she asked.

I nodded. "Tell him it's Maggie from the gym."

Her face scrunched into a frown. What was that look for? Had he told her about me?

"One minute please." She held up her index finger and grabbed the phone. She turned her body away from us as she talked, lowering her voice.

"He'll be right with you. Please have a seat if you'd like," she said after she'd turned around to face us again.

Dorothy and I stepped over into the lobby area, but I didn't sit down. After a few seconds, Keith walked into the lobby. He smiled widely when he saw me.

"It's nice to see you, Maggie. What brings you by today?" he asked with a smile in his tone.

I furrowed my brow. He thought he was so clever. I wasn't the one falling off treadmills though, so who was the clever one?

I crossed my arms in front of my chest and asked. "Why didn't you tell me who you were?"

"You didn't ask," he said with a smile.

That was the lamest answer I'd ever heard. "Don't give me that crap. You could have told me when you found out that I was a P.I., but you didn't. Why not?"

"Yeah, why not?" Dorothy asked with a scowl.

"I had a job to do for my client. I just felt that it was best if no one knew what I was doing."

I stared at him for a couple seconds. "Well, I guess I can buy that, but why were you at the gym? If you were taking photos of Matt's wife, why did you go to that gym?"

I'd find out what info he had on Chuck. I'd been trying to get more information on the relationship between Chuck and Matt Cooper, and Keith just might be my key. Keith glanced over his shoulder at the receptionist, then looked back at me.

He lowered his voice and said, "I think Chuck Moore killed Arthur Abbott."

He could have punched me in the stomach and it wouldn't have felt any different.

"That's exactly what I've been thinking," I said. "But I thought you said you didn't know his last name?"

"Yeah, I just found out."

Dorothy popped a peppermint into her mouth and shoved one into my hand.

After placing the mint in my mouth, I continued, "I need to find the proof. They still have my client in jail for the crime."

Keith nodded. "I'm aware of that."

"Have you been following me too?"

"No, I haven't been following you. Has someone been following you?" he asked.

"Several people have been following us," Dorothy answered for me.

He stared at Dorothy.

"This is my assistant, Dorothy. You remember her from the gym?" I asked.

"Yes, of course." He smiled. "Nice to see you again."

She nodded.

"It's Chuck and a couple other muscle men from the gym who followed me," I said.

"They even left a threatening note on her car," Dorothy offered.

"Are you serious?" Keith asked.

I waved my hand dismissively. "Yes, it was silly really ... something right out of some lame crime caper movie."

"Nonetheless, it's still a serious matter," Keith said.

"That's what I told her, but she doesn't listen to me," Dorothy said.

"Was that you in the park giving the photos to Mr. Louis?" I asked.

He nodded. "It was an associate of mine."

"Well, he followed me. What was that all about?" I asked.

Keith frowned. "I wasn't aware that had happened, but I'll make sure to find out why."

"Are you going to share the info you have with me now? Or do we have to do this the hard way?" I asked crossing my arms in front of my chest.

"Well, no, I'd rather not do this the hard way," he said with a chuckle.

"Good. I'm glad you see it my way."

"Matt Cooper has been taking bribes and so has a judge. I just don't have sufficient proof yet."

"How was that related to the death of Arthur Abbott?" I asked.

"Arthur was going to the authorities with that information. That on top of the fact that Arthur was cheating with Matt's wife was enough to send him over the edge," Keith said.

I released a deep breath. "Too bad I couldn't have discovered this information."

"I've been working on this case for a long time." Keith must have seen the look of disappointment on my face.

Where was Matt's wife? I had questions to ask her. Of course, there was little chance she'd be truthful about her affair. But she could give me more insight into Arthur's relationship with his law firm partners. Matt hadn't wanted to get involved by telling Arthur about his wife's affair with Sam because Arthur was in the same situation with Matt's wife. How would I find her?

Chapter Twenty-Six

"Where are we headed?" Dorothy asked, then popped a peppermint into her mouth.

"The Dolphin Swim and Tennis Club," I offered while navigating a turn.

She scowled. "Isn't that a private club?"

I shrugged. "Since when did I let anything like that stop me? We can tell them that we're interested and possibly want to join the club. They'll give us a tour and we can snoop around for Mrs. Cooper."

"Do you know what she looks like?" Dorothy asked.

I tapped my purse. "I have a photo inside. Take a look."

She pulled out the photo and studied it, then turned to me and said, "I hope I don't really have to join that club. You don't pay me enough to afford it."

I patted her hand. "Don't worry, Dorothy. I'll take care of everything."

We parked outside the posh-looking club. The landscaping was lush and palm trees surrounded the area.

"We'll just tell them you are my grandmother," I said as I climbed out of the car.

When I glanced over, Dorothy was sending me a death glare.

"We'll tell them you are my mother?" I asked.

She scowled again.

"We'll tell them you are my sister?" That was my final offer.

She gave a grin. "Okay, I guess that'll have to do."

When we stepped inside the club, I was completely lost. People milled around, not glancing up at us. They obviously knew what they were doing, but I had no idea where to go. Finally, I spotted the front desk and headed that way with Dorothy hot on my heels.

"We're here for a tour of the club," I told the blonde-haired woman behind the desk.

"Sure, welcome to Dolphin Swim and Tennis Club. If you'll just fill out this card, I'll show you around." She offered a huge smile and handed me a clipboard.

"How do you intend to find her in this huge place?" Dorothy whispered.

"We'll ask around." I waved my hand through the air. "It's probably not as big as it looks."

"I still don't understand. Even if you find her, what are you going to say?"

"I'll ask her about her affair. I want to know what was going on inside that law firm. Allison doesn't have any more info." I finished the information card and clipped the pen back onto the board.

"What makes you think she will tell you?" Dorothy asked.

I shrugged. "I don't, but it's worth a shot."

I stepped back over to the desk and handed the woman the card.

She peered down at the information and said, "It's nice to meet you, Ms. Thomas. I'm happy to show you and your grandmother around the club. Please follow me and we'll get started."

"Ouch!" I said, hopping on one foot and holding my shin with my hand. "Was it really necessary to get violent?"

"I was supposed to be your sister," Dorothy said through gritted teeth.

"Oops, I forgot," I said with a devilish smile.

Our tour guide was in front of us, droning on about the benefits of the club. She had no idea that we weren't paying the least bit of attention. "When she's not looking, we lose her," I whispered to Dorothy.

"You can't be serious." Dorothy frowned.

I quirked my eyebrow. "Dead serious. We'll slip into the women's locker room."

Our guide walked past the door marked as the women's locker room, so as soon as we approached, I opened the door and dragged Dorothy in with me. As we stepped farther into the locker room, I stepped over to a woman who looked approachable and pulled out the photo. Yes, I realize that was probably a creepy move, but I had no other options.

"Have you seen this woman?" I asked.

The woman glared at me, then looked down at the photo. She didn't reply, but instead went back to applying her lipstick.

"Can you just tell me if you've seen her?" I pressed.

She looked at me through the mirror. The scowl on her face remained. She would probably have us thrown out of there at any second.

Finally, she looked over at me again. "Yes, I've seen her." She pointed toward the tennis courts.

I looked in the direction of her pointing finger. "Thank you," I said softly.

When I started to walk away, she grabbed my arm. "What do you want with her?"

I sucked in a deep breath. "It's official business."

"It's because she didn't pay her dues, isn't it?" she said with enthusiasm.

I frowned. "What? I have no . . ."

"I knew they were having money problems. It's a shame." She shook her head.

By the look on this woman's face, I didn't think she was all that sincere about her statement. What made her think that the Coopers were having financial problems? Yet another mystery to unravel, although I doubted it was important to this situation.

"Thank you for the information," I said, and then hurried away.

We made our way outside and toward the tennis courts. The sky was brilliantly blue sprinkled with fluffy white clouds. There was a café area by the courts. I scanned it, looking for the woman.

Just when I was about to give up, Dorothy pointed and said, "Is that her?"

I looked in the direction of her pointing finger. "At that table of women?"

"Yes, the woman in the white blouse."

"Yes, that's her. Good eyes, Dorothy." I motioned for her to follow my lead.

"I don't take vitamin B for nothing, you know," she said with a snort.

"Let's go have lunch," I said.

Dorothy shook her head. "Something tells me this won't end well."

"Oh, what's the worst that could happen?"

We stood at the café's entrance waiting for the hostess to seat us. I was sure she'd seen us standing there. Dorothy started coughing and the woman finally approached.

"We'd like a table, please," I said, looking around at the empty tables.

"Are you members?" she asked looking us up and down.

"We're standing in here, aren't we?" Dorothy quipped.

The hostess stared for a moment and then said, "Just a minute please."

"We are going to get caught. And don't think for one minute I am going down with you, missy. I will act like I don't know you." Dorothy warned with a wave of her finger. "They will believe the old lady over you any day."

The hostess led us across the room. I wasn't exactly dressed appropriately for this place, and by the looks from the women sitting around, they thought so, too. We were seated at the table right beside Matt's wife and her friends.

I took a sip of water and pretended that I was looking at something else as I glanced back to check out the women. The brunette with the bob frowned when she noticed me staring. I whipped back around quickly.

"Well, that was a real smooth move," Dorothy retorted.

I scowled. "I'm trying my best." I leaned back, straining to overhear their conversation.

"Aren't you going to confront her?" Dorothy asked.

I shook my head.

She frowned. "Well, what are you going to do now?"

"I'll think of something. Just give me a second." I tapped my finger against the table, then took another bite of my breadstick.

Dorothy acted as if I was supposed to come up with some grand plan right away.

"You're pressuring me. Stop staring," I said.

When I heard Matt's name mentioned again, I leaned back farther. My chair tipped back and I grabbed the table to keep from crashing onto my butt. The table shook and our water glasses splashed across the pretty white tablecloth.

"I can't take you anywhere," Dorothy fumed.

I straightened in the chair and attempted to regain my composure. Everyone in the place was staring at me. Hadn't they ever seen a woman almost fall out of her chair before? Of course the women at the table behind us were whispering about me. I heard a

giggle and then a description of my frazzled hair. Hey, the humidity was killer.

After the commotion died down, the café returned to normal. My face was still red, though. Dorothy and I finished our meal. Well, I tried to eat, but I'd been distracted and had only taken a few bites. When the women left their table, we got up and followed them. The waiter rushed over and I figured he was chasing me because I'd left such a lousy tip. But it had been all that I could afford.

"You forgot your purse," he said as he shoved my little bag toward me.

I grabbed it without looking. "Thanks."

The women walked inside the building and I knew we had to go after them. Wherever they went, I was going to follow. They glanced around a few times, and I knew they were suspicious of why we were following them. When they looked back again, I stopped, pretending to study a photo on the wall.

"Oh, that was real smooth. I'm sure they didn't suspect you at all."

"Be quiet," I whispered. "Don't look now, but I think we're about to get in trouble."

Our guide was looking for us. I saw her scanning the room. I grabbed Dorothy's arm and rushed her down the hallway. The women had stepped into the locker room, so I pushed Dorothy through the door and inside the room. The women scowled when they spotted us, but they didn't say anything about the fact that we were now in the room with them.

I noticed Matt's wife at the back of the room. She was standing alone, so I knew this was my chance to approach her. What did I have to lose now? I had already broken all the rules by chasing her around the club.

I walked up and said, "Excuse me."

She whipped around and said, “Are you following me?”

She looked like she was ready to take a karate stance. I didn’t know karate, so she might have been able to take me down with one move. I’d have to take a few classes.

“No, I’m not following you. I’m sorry to bother you.”

“Then what do you want?”

“I just need to ask you a few questions, if you don’t mind.”

“Well, I do mind,” she said, grabbing a towel and walking away.

I followed her across the room as she hurried her steps.

“I don’t think you should do that. She’s getting ready to let you have it,” Dorothy said as she rushed behind me.

“Yeah, I know, but I can’t stop now.”

When she stopped in front of the mirror, I knew I had to explain who I was and what I wanted.

“Why should I talk to you?” She continued to stuff things into her bag.

She looked upset and as if she really did want to talk to me. “If you’ll excuse me, I have somewhere I have to be.”

“It’ll just take a moment and it’s very important. You don’t want an innocent woman to go to jail for life, do you?” I asked.

She paused and let out a deep breath. “No, I don’t. Look,” she lowered her voice. “I’m trying to work this out with my husband. Matt isn’t who I thought he was. He wouldn’t let me break off the affair.”

My eyes widened. “What do you mean?”

She looked around to see if anyone was listening. The other women had already left the room. “Matt threatened me. It wasn’t just physical. He threatened to get rid of Arthur if I ended the affair . . . He meant get rid of him financially, of course.”

I hadn’t expected that revelation, but at the same time I wasn’t surprised. If she was fearful and suspected something strange was going on, then it was most likely true. After all, she had the inside info. Now I just needed to figure out what to do with the details I’d uncovered.

I'd just started to respond when someone approached, pulling me out of the conversation.

"There you two are. I've been looking all over for you. I started to think you were just playing games with me." Our tour guide gave a forced smile

I snorted. "Of course not. We'd love to join."

Dorothy poked me in the side. "Ouch. What my much older sister wanted to ask is if you give a senior discount."

The woman smiled from ear to ear. "Of course. Let me just get the paperwork."

When she turned and walked down the hall, I glanced over my shoulder. Mrs. Cooper had disappeared. Dorothy turned to face me. If looks could kill, I'd be at the bottom of that pool down the hall.

"I told you I didn't want to join."

"We're not. Come on." I tugged on her arm and rushed toward the door before the woman came back.

I felt bad about lying to our tour guide, but it had been completely necessary. Hey, maybe someday I really would join the club.

Chapter Twenty-Seven

The next day I headed toward the restaurant on the beach. The card I'd found at the boat dock had two addresses written down. One of them had a street number and the other one didn't. When I looked up the address with the number, I found out it was a restaurant. It was the same restaurant that Allison had told me Matt and Arthur had eaten at the day before Arthur's death—the one I'd forgotten to check out. It would be a long shot, but maybe if I went there I could show Arthur's picture and it would net me some clues.

The air was hot and muggy as I walked across the wooden boardwalk to the restaurant. The restaurant sat right on the beach. It looked like an old weathered beach house, but it had obviously been around for only a few years. The walls were covered with every beach-themed item possible. Fishing nets, palm trees, flip-flops, and surfboards just to name a few. It looked more like a sports bar with multiple TVs all tuned in to a different sporting event.

A quick look at the menu posted on the wall by the door let me know that they served sandwiches, seafood, and beer. The walls facing the beach were all open-air, allowing the breeze and the smell of the ocean to waft through the space. The place was empty except for a couple at a table across the room and a guy on the same side toward the back of the restaurant. He looked up at me when I entered, but the couple was too engrossed in their conversation to notice that anyone else was around.

I sat down at the table closest to the door. I figured while I was there I might as well have lunch. The waitress might be more likely to help me out if she knew I was a paying customer. The tables were made out of the same weather-beaten wood as the walls. There were four stools around each table. I pulled one out and sat down. I knew the odds that I'd find any information were slim, but I had to try everything I could think of. I couldn't just wait for the case to solve itself. I looked around the room for an employee. The woman at the back of the room noticed me and held up her index finger.

The waitress came over with a menu and water.

"Welcome to Beach Bob's Grill. Do you need a minute to look over the menu?" she asked with a bright smile.

I glanced down at the plastic-covered menu. Since it had only a few options, I knew that there was no real debate.

"I'll just take a burger and fries. Water is fine to drink." I nodded.

She grabbed the menu with a smile and hurried away. I busied myself looking over my notes in my iPhone while I waited. The app for the private eye didn't have as much information as I'd hoped. Actually, the app had turned out to be nothing more than a way to take notes. I could have done that with a pen and paper. Maybe I could design my own app in the future. After another couple minutes the waitress returned.

She placed the plate down in front of me. "Can I get anything else for you?

"I could use another napkin." Why was I stalling?

She smiled and handed me another napkin from her apron. "Anything else?" she asked.

"Well, there was just one more thing. Did you happen to work Thursday night? I'm looking for information about a couple of men who were in here."

"Are you a cop?" she asked, looking at me with curiosity.

I shook my head and reached for a business card from my purse. "I'm a private investigator."

Her eyes widened. "I'm not sure if I can help you. We have a lot of customers."

I nodded. "Yeah, I'm sure you do." I pulled out a picture of Arthur and handed it to her. "Have you seen this man?"

She looked at the picture and didn't waste any time nodding. "Yes, I know him. He comes in here a lot. Did he do something wrong?"

I hesitated then finally said, "He's dead."

She covered her mouth with her hand. "Oh my gosh. That's terrible. What happened to him?"

"He was murdered," I said.

Her face turned white. "I'm sorry to hear that. Are you trying to find his killer?"

Trying was the key word in that question. Yes, I was trying, but doing a bad job of it.

"Yes, I am. He was in here with another man the other night," I said.

She nodded. "Yes, I remember seeing them, but they weren't my table that night."

"Do you know who waited on them?" I asked.

"Yes. Monica, but she's not here right now. She'll be here later tonight," she said.

I nodded. "Okay, thanks. Do you think she'll talk to me?"

"I don't see why not," she said.

"Do you remember anything unusual about their time here the other night?" I asked.

She shook her head. "Not really. I guess once I looked over and noticed that their conversation may have been a little animated, but I thought maybe they'd just had a couple beers."

"Thanks again. I'll make sure to come back and talk to Monica," I said.

"Let me know if you need anything else," she said and then walked away.

A guy with blond hair bleached by the sun watched me from the table across the room. Did I have ketchup on my face? After another moment, he got up and headed my way. He wore a T-shirt with a surfboard on the front and long, baggy shorts. He had a lopsided grin on his face the whole time and watched me as he walked.

I glanced over my shoulder, thinking that maybe he was looking at someone behind me, but when he approached my table and stopped, I knew that I was the focus of his attention.

"Hey, I noticed you from across the room," he said when he approached.

"Okay?" I said.

Maybe it was mustard on my face instead of ketchup.

When I stared at him in silence, he finally pointed to my waist. "Are you a cop?"

I glanced down and saw a little bit of my gun peeking out from my shirt.

I looked up at him. "No, I'm a private investigator."

He sat down on the stool across from me. I stared at him.

"Please have a seat," I said sarcastically.

He chuckled, failing to hear the sarcasm in my tone. Or if had, he chose to ignore it.

"Can I buy you a beer?" he asked.

"I'm sorry, but it's a little too early for a beer. Thanks anyway, though," I said.

"Do you come here often?" he asked as I stuffed a french fry into my mouth.

I shook my head. "No, this is the first time." It was the oldest pickup line in existence.

"You should come back more often," he said with a smile.

I never claimed to catch on quickly, but I'd finally figured out why he'd come over. He was flirting. How clueless could I be?

"I take it that you come here often?" I asked.

He shook his head. "Yeah, I hang out here a lot. I used to work here."

"What do you do now?" I asked.

I really didn't want to know, but it seemed like I wasn't going to get out of this without a little bit of conversation with him.

"Well, I am in between jobs. I spend a lot of time surfing," he said.

I stared at him for a minute, then said, "Maybe you could get a job that involves surfing, like working at a surf shop?"

He laughed. I was being completely serious, but who was I to give advice? Heck, I didn't know the first thing about surfing. I could barely swim. Enough of the small talk, though. I needed to find out if he knew anything and then get out of here. Lunchtime was over.

"Did you happen to be here on Tuesday night?" I asked.

He scratched his head. It looked as if he was scrolling through the week's activities in his mind. "Yeah, as a matter of fact, I was. It was the NBA playoffs. Miami Heat was playing, you know?"

I nodded. No, I really didn't know, but that was neither here nor there. I pulled out the picture of Arthur again and slid it across the table. "Do you recognize this man? Apparently he came in here a lot too."

He picked up the photo and I saw the same look of recognition in his eyes as the waitress had had.

"Yeah, I know this dude. He was in here with another man who I'd never seen him with before. They were both wearing suits. Well, this dude always wears a suit, which is kind of odd for the beach."

"Well, he was a lawyer. Maybe he came here after court." I said.

He ran his hand through his hair. "Yeah, that makes sense. What do you want with him?"

Everyone immediately thought that Arthur had done something wrong.

"He was murdered and I'm looking for his killer," I said.

"Get out. How did they kill him?" he asked.

He was crazy if he thought I was going into the gory details.

"I can't release that information, sorry," I said.

Never mind that I wasn't entirely sure myself.

He shrugged. "That's cool."

"So did you happen to hear what the men were talking about?" I asked.

He grabbed one of my french fries and popped it into his mouth. With a mouth full of food, he said, "No, I know the one dude got up and left before their food arrived. He threw down a few bills for his beer and took off."

I straightened on the stool. "Really? So they had an argument?"

He shrugged. "I can't say it was an argument, but it didn't seem like they were happy."

I jumped up and tossed a few bills onto the table. "Thanks for the info. And good luck with the surfing."

It appeared that Matt Cooper had a motive for Arthur's murder and now I knew for sure that they'd been together on the night before.

Chapter Twenty-Eight

Later that evening, I'd picked up Dorothy and we were headed to Matt Cooper's home. Now that I knew Matt's wife was having an affair, I wanted to talk with her more. She'd disappeared before I'd gotten a chance to ask all the questions I had for her. Dorothy and I pulled up to Matt's house. Landscape lighting highlighted the palm trees that surrounded the home. Pathway lights guided people toward the front door. I hadn't expected so many people to be at his home. As a matter of fact, I hadn't expected to see anyone, actually. I had hoped to see something happen, but when snooping, there were no guarantees.

"It looks like they're having a party," Dorothy said, craning her head to get a good look at the guests walking toward the house.

People were dressed in formal attire, so I knew this wasn't an impromptu get-together. One good thing about all the people being around was that I felt like we could blend in with the crowd. No one would pay attention to us, although we weren't exactly dressed for a black-tie event. Cars filled the driveway and even started to line up along the street. My plan definitely hadn't included this scenario, so I wasn't sure what to do.

The sun was setting quickly and I was thankful for the cover of the dark night sky. We watched in silence for another couple minutes. I could have just driven away, but I was too curious. I had to know what was going on inside that house. Why were they

having a party? Was it a special occasion? Why was it so formal? There was only one option for us. I tapped my fingers against the steering wheel as I tried to come up with the best plan. Dorothy grabbed my hand to stop the sound; it was obviously annoying the heck out of her.

Finally, I looked at her and said, "I think we should crash the party."

Her eyes widened as she stared at me. "I think we're a little underdressed, don't you think?" She glared at me.

I looked down at my pink tank top and shorts and over at her Hawaiian shirt. Okay, I was wrong: we would stand out a little, but I couldn't let a little detail like that get in my way.

"Maybe we can peek in the windows," I said.

"Isn't that illegal?" She raised her eyebrow.

I thought about the question for a second. "Hmm. I'm not so sure that party snooping would be illegal. If the police came they would just think we were displaced guests."

Dorothy frowned. "I don't know."

I grabbed the keys from the ignition and opened the door. "Let's give it a shot. You know you want to, Dorothy."

She shook her head. "I don't have a good feeling about this."

I marched toward the house, trying to act completely normal. If Matt Cooper confronted me about being at his party, well, I would just tell him that I had been invited by someone else. It looked as if all the guests had arrived and no one was late for the party.

Dorothy had been fidgeting during the entire walk up the driveway.

"We'll go around to the side of the house and take a look," I said.

"I don't see what good that will do. What do you think you'll discover by peeking in the windows? What kind of food they're serving?" Dorothy said.

I shrugged. "I don't know. I never claimed to have all the answers. Maybe I'll get some kind of clue as to what the party is for."

"Oh, you're just nosy," she said.

"I'm going to ignore that," I said.

As we approached the house, someone called out to me. "You're late and the help goes in the side entrance over here."

I whirled around to find a woman standing behind us. She had a scowl on her face and her hands firmly on her hips.

"Now get in there and get to work, both of you. The food is ready to be served. I hope you brought your change of clothing. You're supposed to wear a white shirt and black pants," she said.

I glanced at Dorothy. She shook her head, but I knew this was a perfect opportunity to get inside the house.

As we followed the woman around to the side entrance, Dorothy whispered, "There is no way I am waiting on these people. My feet will hurt. I didn't sign up for this."

"Well, I didn't, either." I said.

When we entered the house, the woman pointed at the bathroom on the left. "You can change in there, but hurry up."

Dorothy snorted. "She is a bossy bitch."

"I have no intention of doing it anyway," I said.

"Besides, we don't have any clothing to change into," Dorothy reminded me.

"Come on, we'll sneak through the house and find out what's going on. Make sure to keep your ears open to see if you overhear anything," I said.

"I don't know what I'm listening for." She shook her head.

Sadly, I had no idea what I was listening for, either. We slipped into the kitchen. The space was full of bodies busy preparing food. Wait staff and chefs crisscrossed in front of each other in a flurry of activity. In the corner of the kitchen, I spotted the boss so I hurried Dorothy into the next room. A few people looked at us when we entered the area full of party guests.

I smiled nervously as I practically carried Dorothy into the room. She was not a good investigative partner tonight. Luckily, people were so busy talking with others that they turned their attention away from us.

"We need to find a corner to hide so we can blend in," I said.

"You think I can blend in with these people? They're wearing clothing that would cost me a year's paycheck." She frowned at me.

"Hey, I pay you a good wage. It's the going rate for assistants," I said.

She rolled her eyes. "No matter."

I didn't have more money to pay her even if I had wanted to give her a raise. "Never mind that right now," I said.

"I'm wearing an orange shirt with purple flowers. I might as well wave a flag and tell everyone to look over at me," she said.

I wasn't much better in my shorts and tank. Women wore elegant dresses and most men wore tuxedos; a few wore suits. In contrast, I was dressed for a picnic.

We inched out into the foyer, making our way further into the belly of the beast. When I neared the living room, I stopped.

"Look at the small sign above the fireplace," I said.

In an understated framed sign above the mantel were the words *Happy Anniversary* with a picture of Matt Cooper and his wife. Well, at least now I knew what the party was for. I instantly felt bad for invading their private event. I really had no business being inside their home, although I had kind of been dragged into the space.

We watched for a few seconds, and then I whispered to Dorothy, "We should just get out of here."

"I think that is the best thing you've said all night," Dorothy said.

I couldn't wait to get home and crash. I had a rerun of *Magnum, P.I.* just waiting for me.

"I am starving. I didn't get a chance to eat dinner before you dragged me to this shindig. You didn't even give me a chance

to get a peppermint out of my purse before we came in here," Dorothy said.

As I stepped back into the foyer, Dorothy stopped a waiter with a tray of food.

"I can't believe they are still having this party," a woman said.

I turned around to look at the man and woman talking next to me. They didn't pay attention to me and didn't notice that I was now eavesdropping. I inched a little closer, hoping to hear more of this juicy conversation.

"I can't believe she was cheating on him," the man said.

What was with everyone cheating at that law firm? Was it something in the water? Did this couple have more information about the affair or did they just like to gossip? Unfortunately, they had changed the topic after they'd grabbed food off the passing tray and were now talking about their upcoming vacation. I wanted to ask them, but I knew it was time for us to get out of there. They must have felt me staring at them because they looked over and frowned. I smiled, but they didn't return the sentiment. I motioned with a tilt of my head for Dorothy to follow me back the way that we'd come. We moved across the foyer again. I could almost see our escape.

"Dorothy Raye? What are you doing here?" a woman said loudly.

I froze on the spot. What would we do now? I hadn't expected anyone to recognize us in a million years. The woman hurried over to Dorothy and at the same time I rushed over to grab her. I was too late, though, because the woman was hugging Dorothy.

"You look great," the woman said.

I could tell she wasn't being sincere.

"We have to get out of here," I whispered to Dorothy as she continued chatting with this woman.

Finally the women said their good-byes and I pulled Dorothy's arm, guiding her through a group of people. As I made it to the

dining room, I smashed right into a man's chest. It almost knocked the wind out of my lungs.

"What the hell are you doing here?" Matt Cooper glared at me.

His face turned red. I expected to see steam coming out of his ears. I hadn't planned on this scenario. But I hadn't thought it *wouldn't* happen, either. Now, as I thought back about the stupid excuse I'd come up with in case I'd run into Matt, I realized it wasn't a very good plan.

"You mean I wasn't invited?" I asked innocently.

When the little vein on his temple appeared, I knew it was time for us to get out of there. I grabbed Dorothy and practically carried her to the back door. The woman who had ushered us inside to work yelled out, but I didn't glance back.

As we hurried around the side of the house, I stumbled around a shrub. Dorothy was ahead of me. I had no idea a woman her age could move that fast. It was as if someone had said they were giving away free yarn.

When I'd almost made it safely to the driveway, a hand grasped my arm and I screamed. Not very tough private eye-like, but it was what it was.

"What the hell are you doing?" I said when I'd turned around and saw who it was. "Why are you always lurking around? Stop following me."

"Did you enjoy the party?" Jake asked.

"What are you doing here?" I pushed him lightly, making contact with his hard chest. "You are crossing the creepy stalker line. No, you've already crossed that line."

"I'm just following up on a few things," he said.

"I find that hard to believe. As a matter of fact, I don't believe you at all." I spun around and continued down the drive toward the car.

Chapter Twenty-Nine

The next morning, waves rolled up to the beach as I walked along the shore. People had marked out their spots with beach towels, ready to soak up the sun all day. I stuck my feet into the water, relishing the coolness against my bare skin. The sun shone bright and warmed my skin. It had been a wild time since Arthur Abbott had walked into my office wanting me to find out if his wife had been cheating. Maybe if I had it to do over I would never have taken the job, although I really did want to help Allison. She didn't deserve to be in jail for a crime she hadn't committed.

I neared the condo towers. Yes, I'd known exactly where I was headed when I set off for a walk down the beach. Looking at the buildings from a different perspective might give me a whole new angle on this thing. It was odd that Jake hadn't been around. I'd gotten so accustomed to him trailing me that I now expected it.

When I reached the towers, I stopped. I knew the police had looked thoroughly around the area, but I held on to some hope that they'd overlooked something. Even if they had, though, the odds of me finding any new clues were slim.

I got shivers down my spine when I looked at the spot where Mr. Shaw's body had washed ashore. When I looked up at the building, someone was watching me. It was the tower where I'd found Arthur's body. The place was supposed to be empty now. Even worse, I thought for sure it was Arthur Abbott's condo.

The watcher was definitely a woman. She appeared to have blonde hair, just like Allison Abbott. Had she gotten out of jail? I had to go find her. With all the stress and my lack of sleep, maybe I'd imagined that I'd see her. That wouldn't be entirely out of the question.

Without waiting another minute, I made my way across the sand to the building. I stepped around a couple basking in the sun, almost tripping on their bottle of suntan lotion. The crime scene tape was still draped over the back entrance. I wouldn't let that stop me from going in. It hadn't stopped me in the past, so I wouldn't let it now. I assumed the police were watching the building after what had happened, but it was a chance I'd have to take.

I glanced around to see if anyone watched me, then slipped under the tape and stepped onto the patio. The building had taken on a new level of creepiness after I'd found the body. The fact that Arthur had stayed here all by himself was weird enough, but now it was like a building straight out of the apocalypse.

Weaving around a lounge chair, I walked up to the back door and tried to open it. It wouldn't budge. I should have expected as much. The back door was locked, but maybe the front would still be unlocked. I'd have to go around to the front. If it was locked then I knew the watcher had to be Allison. How had she gotten out of jail? She would have a key to the place, right? There was only one way in at this point, so whomever I saw, I'd surely find them at the front entrance if they tried to get away. I made my way across the patio again, slipped under the tape, and looked around. Still no one seemed to notice me. I eased through the sand and around the building.

When I reached the front door of the building, I peered around, looking for any sign of movement. I was still a little paranoid after being shot at. If the police were truly watching the building, they must be asleep.

I pushed on the door, but it was locked too. I looked up as if that would offer some clue. As I suspected, it did not. The woman must have slipped back down and locked the door behind her. Or maybe she was still in the building and had locked it behind her when she went in. I could wait for a while to see if she came out. If that had been Allison, though, she would have come down to find me. She would have wanted to talk to me. Heck, she would have already tried to call me. I pulled my phone out and checked to see if I'd missed a call.

As I stood there peering up at the building, wondering what to do next, footsteps sounded from behind me. I whipped around and let out a tiny yelp. He had scared me.

"May I help you?" the police officer asked in a stern voice.

Oh, great. I was going to be arrested for trespassing. "I was just looking at the building," I said, although my words came out more of a question than a statement.

My voice didn't sound very confident.

He frowned. "You're not supposed to be here."

"It's okay, Officer Marquez. She's with me."

I glanced over my shoulder and saw Jake's familiar smile. I couldn't hide my smile in return. The officer nodded and walked away.

"Are you trying to get arrested?" he asked with a grin.

"Well, not exactly. I was just taking a walk along the beach," I said.

He finished my sentence for me. "And you just happened to pass by."

I stared. "Yeah, something like that."

"Are you going to tell me why you were really here?" His mouth twisted up at the corners.

"Are you going to tell me why you're here? It seems as if you're still following me." I crossed my arms in front of my chest.

"I'm not following you. I was just here on official business." He gestured over his shoulder.

"If you say so. Listen, I saw someone in Arthur Abbott's condo." I scanned the area for the woman, but noticed only Officer Marquez watching us.

He raised an eyebrow. "You were up there?"

I ran my hand through my hair. "No, I saw the person looking out the window when I was on the beach."

His lips curled up. "I doubt that, because the doors are locked. No one was up there unless an officer went up with them. I'll check it out."

I knew he didn't believe me.

Jake walked toward the condo tower and I followed. Just then, we saw the woman rush around the side of the building. What was she doing? Was it Allison?

I pointed. "There she is. Did you see her?"

He nodded and took off after her.

"Hey, stop right there," Jake called out.

The woman glanced back and I finally realized that it wasn't Allison. It was the wife of Thomas Shaw. It made sense that she would be at the condos, but why had she been in Arthur Abbott's place? I knew she'd looked familiar. I'd seen her at the salon.

Jake stopped the woman. "Ma'am, what are you doing here? Is everything okay?"

"If it wasn't for that damn condo, my husband would be alive right now. I told him to just let it go," the woman said.

"Let me walk you to your car." Jake guided her toward the parking lot.

Jake nodded for me to wait for him while he helped the woman. I needed to find out what she meant. I was pretty sure she was talking about the issue with Arthur's condo, but there was no way I could get to her with Jake around. I'd have to pay her a visit later. I walked around to the patio to wait for Jake.

The air was hot and the sun was blazing down on me, so I decided to walk down to the water and wait for Jake. When

I reached the beach, I slipped off my sandals and let my feet sink into the sand. It squished between my toes and was relatively cool considering how hot it was in the middle of the day. It felt good under my feet.

A few people walked up and down the shoreline, but it was mostly empty in front of the condo and very peaceful. I tuned out my surroundings, allowing in only the sound of the waves lapping against the shore. Of course in the distance I heard the traffic, but out there by the water, it seemed like a different world.

Without thinking, I took off down the beach, splashing my feet in the water as I went along. I didn't plan on walking too far—just enough to relax and cool off so that maybe I could clear my thoughts. It was no wonder I hadn't been sleeping well with all the thoughts taking up space in my mind. I needed to relax and stop thinking about the case for a few minutes, but that was easier said than done.

As I moved down the beach, a strange sensation overcame me, and it wasn't fear of a jellyfish or Jaws. No, this was something bigger than that. It felt as if someone was walking behind me. I glanced over my shoulder every few minutes, but didn't notice anything. It was my mind playing tricks on me.

When I glanced back again, he was standing right behind me. I jumped and clutched my chest.

"Okay, that is creepy as hell. I'm beginning to think you're a stalker. What is wrong with you?" I clutched my chest.

Jake Jackson was behind me with that sexy grin on his face again. I was pretty sure he was enjoying being a pain in my ass.

"Can't a guy walk on the beach?" he asked.

"Yes, a guy can, but do you have to sneak up on me like that?"

"It's how I move," he said with a small curve of his lips.

I wasn't even going to touch that comment.

"What's going on?" I asked.

"It looks like we're going for a walk on the beach." The cadence of his voice sent an odd jolt to the pit of my stomach.

I turned around and continued my walk. Of course Jake hurried his pace and caught up to me. He matched my stride and walked along beside me. His skin was bronzed from the sun as if he'd spent many hours on the beach, maybe catching a few waves on his surfboard.

"It's a beautiful day," he said, looking up at the cloudless sky. "I thought it might rain earlier, but I'm glad the clouds gave way."

So he was here to discuss the weather with me? I glanced over at him and I knew he must have read my mind. "You don't want to talk about the weather?"

Jake's spicy scent drifted across the breeze. "What do you want to talk about?"

"How about what that woman said back there?" I asked.

"You really don't want me around, do you?" he said with a playful smile.

"I don't think I have a choice." I splashed the water with my foot.

He ran his hand through his thick hair. "Sure. If you want me to get lost, just say the word."

As much as my head screamed for me to tell him to get lost, I remained silent. Nothing came out and with my silence, his smile widened, which in turn made my stomach dance.

"We're looking into what the woman said. I promise." He crossed his chest with his index finger.

That was a start, but it wasn't good enough for me. I'd have to find out what she meant on my own.

Chapter Thirty

After leaving the beach, I'd picked up Dorothy. I hadn't counted on spotting my muscle man stalker sitting outside my office building. The guy had been stupid enough to fall asleep behind the wheel. I supposed he'd been waiting for me. After we'd been sitting in my car for just a few minutes, the genius had woken up and decided to leave. That was when we merged onto the highway and followed his car through the streets of Miami, weaving in and out of traffic.

"Wherever he goes, we're going to follow him," I said.

Dorothy waved her hands through the air. "I agree with you. For once and for all we need to get to the bottom of this and find out what he wants. I'll take him down with my pocketbook. I'm not going to put up with this guy trying to intimidate us."

"I don't think you'll have to attack him with your purse." I took the next right, following his car as closely as possible without being noticed.

I had to do a lot of crazy driving, but I'd managed to keep up with the car as it turned into a parking lot. Neon lights from various nightclubs flashed up ahead and I had a suspicion that he was going to one of those clubs. No matter, I would follow him wherever he went. I'd go into the men's restroom after him if that was what it took.

After following the car into the parking lot, we watched as Chuck Moore pulled up in front of the club. There was something

unusual about this club, though. There were only men walking in. Where were all the women? Then when I looked over at the side of the building and saw a photo of women wearing bikinis, I knew that all the women were already inside the place, dancing for the men's entertainment. The words *Sin Den* flashed in neon letters above the door.

Dorothy was watching all the action, but based on her silence, I figured she hadn't realized what kind of club this was yet. It would only be a matter of time. I would just have her wait in the car because I knew I had to go in after this guy.

So what if it wasn't the kind of place I would ever frequent of my own volition? I could handle this, right? What was the big deal? Women would be dancing; I had seen women before. Heck, I was one. I'd just make sure not to touch anything that the men had touched, because, well, I had no idea where their hands had been. Good thing I kept hand sanitizer in my purse. Did the guys touch themselves while in the club? That was against the rules or something, right? The bouncers would kick them out for that kind of stuff, right? Heck, I had no idea what went on and it really didn't matter right now. All I needed to know was why this creep was following me and who had sent him. I circled the parking lot until I finally found a spot. The place was packed. At least maybe I'd go unnoticed.

This was the job. I had to suck it up.

"What a minute. I know what kind of place this is," Dorothy said in a loud voice. "It's a burlesque show."

I snorted. "Yeah, I guess you could call it that."

I shoved the car into park and turned off the ignition. At least Jake wouldn't know what I was doing. I glanced in the rearview mirror. Or would he? I didn't think he had followed me, but he had a special knack for sneaking up on me. He was good like that. If he saw me at the Sin Den, I'd never live it down.

"We can't go into that club," Dorothy said.

"We don't have any other options." I avoided her glare, but I felt her eyes fixed on me.

"Oh, we have lots of options." Irritation filled her voice.

I sighed. "You know what I mean. Why don't you stay in the car and I'll slip in real quick?"

"No way, I'm going into the club with you. I can't let you go in there on your own with all those men."

I had a vision of Dorothy swinging her pocketbook around if anyone said anything out of order. Meanwhile, my guy slipped into the club, so I knew I didn't have time to argue with her about going with me.

"Okay, let's get this over with." I motioned for her to follow.

Dorothy and I hurried across the parking lot. I had on my shorts and sandals and she had on her linen pants and orthopedic shoes. We were so out of place it wasn't even funny. The bouncer's eyes grew wide when we walked in the door. I was sure he'd never seen two women like us come into the club before.

"Is this your grandmother?" he asked, looking at us with a smirk.

"As a matter of fact, I am." Dorothy smirked back.

He shrugged. "Whatever floats your boat."

He waved us through.

"Aren't you going to check my ID?" I asked.

He looked me up and down. "No, I think you're fine."

We stepped into the dark club. I'd never been in one before, had only seen strip clubs on television. Women danced around poles and men surrounded the stage as music pumped. Yeah, it looked the same as on TV. It was so crowded. How would I ever find this man? I'd have to ask around, but who would I ask? Everyone looked a little busy.

We stepped over to the bar and attempted to hide in the corner.

"Can I get you something?" a voice asked from over my shoulder.

I turned around to find a woman in a blue bikini staring at me. My eyes widened.

"Would you like something to drink?" she pressed.

I shook my head. "No, we're good." I waved her away.

"You should have asked her where the creep was," Dorothy said.

Yeah, she did have a point; I should have asked.

Dorothy's eyes were popping out of her head. "Those girls don't have any clothes on."

"Well, yeah, Dorothy, that's why they call it a strip club. They strip off all their clothing." I looked up, trying to make eye contact only, avoiding looking at anyone from the neck down. "Let's just find this guy and get out of here."

"Hey, honey, are you dancing?" a middle-aged guy asked.

Dorothy scowled and waved her pocketbook at him. The guy looked stunned that she'd tried to attack him with her gigantic bag. He moved back a couple steps to miss her swinging purse.

"What would your mama think about you talking to a lady like that?" Dorothy demanded.

He frowned and pointed at me. "Hey, she's in the club, ain't she?"

"That doesn't make any difference and you need to watch your behavior." She warned with a wave of her index finger. "What's your mama's name? I might just call her."

I grabbed Dorothy's arm and steered her away from the guy. "Don't pay any attention to that guy, Dorothy. He's probably drunk."

"Well, he needs to learn his manners." She adjusted her clothing and patted down her frazzled hair.

I couldn't argue with that assessment. Dorothy and I hurried away from the man and back over to the corner of the room. We might be safe there, hidden away from the movement of the crowd. The thumping of the music and the ruckus of the crowd were giving me a headache. Besides, it was beginning to look hopeless, and

I wanted to get out of there. I'd give it just a couple more minutes and then we were leaving.

The waitress frowned at us. I knew what she was thinking. Heck, I was asking myself the same question now that we were actually in the club.

"You two don't look like you belong in here. Are you lost?" she furrowed her brow as she studied my face.

I smiled. "No, I'm not lost, but I'm actually looking for someone."

She adjusted her tray and looked at me. "Oh yeah? Who are you looking for?"

"Well, he's a guy with big muscles and dark hair." I showed his size with my hands.

She chuckled. "Well, that doesn't narrow it down much. There are a lot of guys who fit that description."

"He has a tattoo on his arm," I said hopefully. "It's a tiger with flames."

Her eyes widened. "I know that guy. He comes in here all the time. And yeah, he was just here tonight. He was sitting over there in the corner." She pointed.

My eyes widened and I looked in the direction of her pointing finger. "Is he still over there?"

She shook her head. "No, I just saw him head out."

Just as she said that, I looked up at the door and spotted the muscle man. He was with another man and I was sure it was Matt Cooper.

I nudged Dorothy. "Look who it is—and look who's with him. We have to go after them."

Dorothy and I weaved through the crowd toward the door.

"I should have known that Matt Cooper was involved with this, and I bet he killed Arthur Abbott too," I said.

"That just sends chills down my spine," Dorothy said as she rubbed her arms. We'd almost made it to the door when the drunk guy appeared again. I thought we'd gotten rid of him.

"I thought I told you to get out of here." Dorothy lunged forward again.

"Hey, grandma, don't tell me what to do," he stuttered.

I wasn't sure what happened next, but I wasn't going to let this guy talk to Dorothy like that. Everything is kind of a blur, but I remember pulling my arm back, then hurling my fist forward to meet his jaw.

He stumbled back, wobbling on his already unsteady feet. My punch had made pretty good contact considering how big the man was. He lurched forward, but I grabbed a chair and threw it at him. In a flash of movement, I grabbed Dorothy's hand and rushed toward the door. Before we made it, though, the bouncers surrounded us.

"There's no fighting allowed," the bigger one said.

"Then why don't you talk to that guy about your policy?" I said through gritted teeth.

"Out you go." The big blond-haired guy motioned, then grabbed my arm.

So now I could add being kicked out of a strip club to the list of crazy things that had happened in my life. The men hadn't been gentle about sending us out the door, either. As we were being kicked out of the club onto our butts, the men entering the club stared at us. I knew how ridiculous we looked.

As angry as I was about the way we'd been treated, and as much as I wanted to complain to the management, I had to push that thought to the back of my mind. I needed to find Chuck Moore and Matt Cooper. I scanned the parking lot, but didn't see the men or their cars.

I released a deep breath and ran my hand through my hair. "We lost them."

"Well, now I can say I've been in a burlesque club," Dorothy said in all seriousness.

"Yeah, that's something I'm sure the Bunco club will find very entertaining," I quipped.

Chapter Thirty-One

The next day I sat at my desk, staring at my computer screen. There were many secret databases that private investigators used. But they cost money and that was something I didn't have a lot of at the moment. I really needed to solve this case so that I could get the rest of the fee from Allison.

After just a little bit of Internet searching, I'd discovered a phone number for Chuck. With any luck it would be his current number. I could ask him if he remembered me.

"Hey, do you remember me? I'm the girl you followed and then found in your apartment. By the way, that *Playgirl* photo must have been Photoshopped."

That was a mean thing to say, but he deserved it for following me around in the first place. If he didn't want harsh critiques, he shouldn't follow women around like a bully. He didn't know who he was messing with when he messed with me, not to mention Dorothy. She was worse than I was.

I dialed the number and held my breath, waiting for someone to answer. I could have gone back to his apartment, but why have a confrontation that would turn ugly for him? I would allow him to avoid bodily harm and just call him on the phone instead. Besides, I didn't need another embarrassing scene of him chasing me with no clothing on.

After several rings, I'd almost given up on anyone answering when a soft female voice said, "Hello?"

Had I dialed the wrong number? Surely, no one who sounded that sweet would be hanging around with this guy.

What information could she provide?

"I'm looking for a Chuck Moore. Do you know him?" I asked, not holding out much hope that I had the right number after all.

Apparently, my private eye skills weren't nearly as good as I'd hoped they'd be by now. I still had a lot to learn. Unfortunately, this wasn't the type of job where you could learn as you went. There was a pause on the other end of the line, but I still heard her breathing.

"Are you there?" I asked, waiting for her to answer.

"I haven't seen him in a while," she answered around a sigh.

"Oh, well, do you have another phone number for him?" I asked, crossing my fingers and hoping that she had a recent one.

"No, obviously he doesn't want to talk to his aunt. He's nothing but trouble," she said, even though I hadn't asked for that information.

"What do you mean?" I pushed.

She probably wouldn't offer any more information, but it was worth asking anyway.

"He's always in trouble with the police. I don't know what's wrong with that boy. If he'd spend as much time trying to stay out of trouble as he does getting into it, we'd all be better off." She released a sigh.

"I'm sorry to hear that," I said softly.

She obviously didn't mind discussing her nephew.

"So you're his aunt?" I asked.

"Who are you?" she demanded.

Uh-oh. I'd crossed the line and pushed for too much information too fast.

"I'm just a friend," I said because I couldn't think of anything else to say.

She snorted as if she figured I was just as much trouble as Chuck since we were friends.

"If you know what's good for you then you'll stay away from him," she warned.

"What is he in trouble for?" I asked.

There was no way she would answer that question, right?

"Oh, you name it, he's done it, I guess. Though I don't think he's murdered anyone yet," she said with a smirk in her voice.

Well, that was a good thing to know, although from the way he'd looked at me when I was in his apartment, I suspected I might end up as his first victim.

"Thank you for the information," I said.

I hadn't got his correct number, but at least I knew a little more information about him. Now I just needed to find out what he had been in court for. Had he been in jail? I was curious to find out what exactly this man had done.

"You're welcome and good luck," she said with a snort and then hung up the phone.

Apparently she felt that I needed that luck. She was probably right.

Unfortunately, it was harder than people thought to find information about someone. I needed to find out who Chuck Moore was and what connection he had to Matt Cooper.

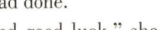

I walked into the courthouse praying that I'd find the information I was looking for, or at the very least, just find something so that I didn't leave empty-handed. After being pointed in the right direction, I found the room where I could get a copy of a person's

criminal record. The woman at the counter took my information and I paid her the fee.

I sat on the chairs lined up against the wall and waited anxiously. I fidgeted and shifted in the seat, checking the time on my phone every few seconds. I peered across the room, but didn't see the woman. I hoped it wouldn't be much longer. An uneasy feeling came over me, and I felt the need to get out of there as quickly as possible. It was like the feeling you get when something is just about to go horribly wrong.

I pushed to my feet and then paced the length of the floor several times. Finally, the woman appeared with the papers in hand. I took them from her, thanked her, then hurried out the door. Once I reached my car, I locked the doors and began looking at this guy's rap sheet. For someone who had been in so much trouble, he'd spent very little time in jail. There was something that jumped out at me right away though. It was like an "ah-ha" moment. Matt Cooper was his lawyer.

I figured I should drive to Mr. Cooper's office and demand an answer right away. It was no coincidence that he was Moore's lawyer and now Moore was following me. He had a lot of explaining to do. There was no other way to explain why this guy had followed me unless Mr. Cooper had asked him to.

By the time I'd left the courthouse, I knew what the connection was between the men and I finally had a reason to believe that Matt Cooper had sent his guy and his fellow goons to hunt me down. But was Sam Louis involved too? Maybe if Matt Cooper had gotten him off from the charges, Chuck owed him a favor. Did that favor include following me? Did it include murdering Arthur Abbott? It was a scary thought, but certainly possible. Apparently Mr. Cooper thought I was a threat. Maybe he knew that I was close to finding out his little secret.

As I headed toward the law firm, I passed Chuck's apartment building and decided to see if he was home. I cruised through the

building's parking lot. Just as I was driving through, Chuck came out of his building. Crap. What would I do now?

I sped up, but not too fast because I didn't want to draw attention to myself. I pulled to the end of the parking lot and turned my car around. I wasn't about to let him go anywhere without following him now that I had him in my sights. He would probably lead me right to Matt Cooper. He eased out of the parking space and pulled out onto the road. So far I didn't think he knew that I was behind him.

As I followed his car through the streets of Miami, I began to wonder if he knew I was following him. It was as if he was just driving in circles. What was he doing? He made a left on the next street, then pulled onto the highway. I followed him another few miles and he merged off the highway. I knew this exit and I had a feeling where he was headed.

Why he'd driven around several blocks before heading to the gym was beyond me. Unless he'd been driving to get rid of me. Fat chance of that ever happening. When he pulled up to the gym and parked, I knew that this had been a wasted trip. I was more furious than ever. I'd had enough and I was going to confront Matt. I would have gone to Jake with what I'd found, but he wouldn't take it seriously anyway, so what was the point?

Chapter Thirty-Two

Matt Cooper still hadn't gotten Allison out of jail or even talked to her, for that matter. I intended to find out why and about his connection with Chuck. When I arrived at the law firm, I spotted Matt leaving the parking lot in his black Mercedes. I immediately followed him. I saw there was another car following Matt too—Jake.

The condo tower parking lot was mostly empty, as usual. Matt turned his car into the lot first, and then, a few car lengths behind him, Jake turned in. Pulling my car up to the curb, I hung back so that neither Matt nor Jake would see my car. What was Jake doing here?

After a few seconds, I moved forward and turned into the lot. Matt had parked and Jake had just pulled into a space nearby. Matt climbed out of his car and moved toward the front door. He never turned around to see that Jake was closing the distance between them.

Stepping out of my car and heading across the parking lot, I watched Jake follow Matt into the empty building. As far as I could tell, Matt had no clue that either of us was watching him. I glanced around the parking lot to see if anyone else had followed us. At least I was aware of my surroundings. Where were the other police? What had happened to the officer who was supposed to be guarding the building? A few pedestrians were on the sidewalk,

but they never looked over to notice me. This situation was making me extremely nervous, to say the least. Shouldn't Jake have called for backup? Did he suspect Matt as well?

When I thought enough time had passed and I wouldn't be noticed, I opened the front entrance door and stepped into the lobby. The men were nowhere in sight, but I heard the ding of the elevator doors. I rushed over in time to see that based on the indicator above the elevator doors, both elevators were headed to the sixth floor. I didn't have time to wait for the elevators to come back, so I pushed through the emergency door and started the long climb up six flights of stairs. After the second flight, I realized that I was crazy for even entertaining the idea of climbing all those stairs. Apparently, I had a death wish. The more I climbed, the longer it seemed. I'd need an oxygen tank by the time I got to the top.

Maybe I should have waited for an elevator. When I finally reached the sixth floor landing, I opened the door and peeked out. I glanced to my left and to my right, but the men weren't there. Maybe I'd gotten the wrong floor. I looked back at the number on the wall. This was the sixth floor, all right.

When I stepped out into the hallway and turned the corner, I saw Matt and Jake. I eased up against the wall, hoping that they wouldn't turn around and notice me. Jake was moving along the wall, trailing Matt. How Jake had gone unnoticed was beyond me.

Unfortunately for me, the floor was tile and my sandals were clicking with each step. I slipped out of my shoes and left them in the hallway. I continued down the long corridor in my bare feet, inching my way along the wall. I finally realized that I'd been holding my breath. I was pausing to release my pent-up breath when Jake stopped.

Matt entered a condo, and within seconds, Jake went in right behind him. He hadn't bothered to knock. Now I had to decide if I was going in too. I inched my way over to the door and paused

with my hand on the doorknob. Pressing my ear against the door, I listened for talking or fighting. Heaven forbid I hear a gunshot. The muffled voices sounded from the other side of the door. I couldn't make out what was being said. The voices grew louder. My heart thumped wildly.

When the sound of banging and then a loud crash rang out, I knew I had to go inside. In one giant movement, I shoved the door open. The sofa and chair had been turned over. I scanned the room and that was when I spotted the men on the balcony. Matt had Jake in a headlock. Jake struggled to break free, then Matt slammed him into the railing. They were dangerously close to the edge. Panic surged through my body. How would I save Jake? I couldn't let Matt toss him over the balcony like a bag of trash.

I pulled out my gun and pointed. So what if my hand was shaking? "Stop or I'll shoot," I yelled.

I honestly never thought I'd utter that phrase. The men froze, both stunned to see me standing there.

"Slowly put your hands up," I demanded as I stared at Matt.

When I glanced over at Jake, his expression was priceless. I knew he was shocked that I'd saved his ass. Why in the hell was he fighting with Matt out there on the balcony?

"You won't shoot," Matt sneered.

I steadied my hand. "The hell I won't, and I've got damn good aim, too. I'd suggest that you not make any sudden moves. Now put your hands up."

Jake turned to Matt, but before Jake could take him down, the balcony railing gave way and Matt fell backward. I rushed over, stopping short of the edge, and peered down. Matt had landed on a tiki bar. The wood and grass had broken his fall. He moved his legs and arms and groaned.

"He's still alive," I said.

Jake looked over the edge. "I'll call for an ambulance." He pulled out his phone and made a quick call for backup.

"We'd better get down there before he gets up and walks away." I said, pointing down at the broken tiki bar.

"I doubt he'll be going anywhere fast for a while." Jake released a deep breath and grabbed my arm. "Are you okay?"

I nodded and released a deep breath. "Yeah, I'm just peachy. How about you?"

"I guess I'm much better now."

I moved across the condo to the front door and Jake followed on my heels. He watched as I paused in the hallway to slip back into my sandals.

"Were you following me?" Jake asked.

As we walked down the hallway, I said, "Yes, I was following you. Well, I wasn't following you at first, I was following Matt, but then you were following him, so it just kind of worked out that way, you know?"

He shook his head. "Yes, I guess I can see how that worked out. Well, thanks. That took a lot of courage." Jake followed dangerously close behind me.

I shrugged. "Just doing my job."

When we reached the elevator, Jake punched the Down button. The light indicted that the car was on the first floor.

"It'll take too long," I said. "We'll have to take the stairs." I motioned over my shoulder as I headed toward the door.

"You've got a lot of spunk, you know that?" Jake said with laughter in his words as he followed me down the stairs.

"You were in a bit of a pickle there for a minute. It's a good thing I came to save the day." I patted him on the back.

I hadn't expected to feel a rush of adrenaline with one simple touch.

"Yeah, it's a good thing," Jake said with a chuckle.

My lack of oxygen must have amused him. But it was a hell of a lot easier to go down than it was to go up. Thank goodness, because I'd need a lung transplant if I had to climb those stairs again.

I'd almost reached the bottom when I lost my sandal. I paused to grab the shoe, then ran to catch up with Jake. After finally reaching the first floor, I rushed past Jake and out into the lobby without even waiting for him

"Slow down, spunky," he said.

I prayed he didn't make that my new nickname. What was I saying? It wasn't like I'd ever see him again after today. There would be no reason to see him again. With Jake right behind me, I rushed out the back door onto the patio area. Jake ran around me and over to the perp. Matt groaned.

As Jake attended to Matt, the sound of sirens grew closer. Finally, the lights flickered from the parking lot and the police rushed back to the patio area.

"What the hell happened?" an older man in a suit asked Jake.

The man looked me up and down. "Oh, it's you."

"I'm sorry, do I know you?" I returned the man's stare.

"No, but I've heard all about you," he said with a quirk of his brow.

I quirked a brow in return. I wasn't even going to touch that subject right now.

"What happened?" He shifted his scrutiny from Jake to me.

"I came in and found Jake and the perp fighting. I instructed the man to freeze as I pulled my gun on him," I recounted the scene matter-of-factly.

The man looked at Jake. Jake shifted his gaze toward the police action—anything to avoid our stares.

"So you saved him?" The officer pointed at Jake.

I knew he was fighting back laughter.

My eyes linked with his. "I guess you could say that."

He snorted as he walked away. Within a few seconds, I'd gotten quite a few looks from the other officers. After giving my statement to the police, I sat on the curb and waited for Jake to finish talking with the other officers. They had already started teasing

him about having the private eye save him. What could I say? It was all in a day's work.

Jake sat down beside me. He smelled good and looked even better. "Thanks for what you did," he said without looking over at me.

"You're welcome," I said softly. "You would have done the same for me, although it was your job to help save me if I was in that situation, but whatever." I chuckled. "Why were you following Matt Cooper?"

"I found the car that had been following you. It belonged to some guy named Chuck Moore. Anyway, I found out that he had a connection to Matt Cooper."

"So you basically listened to me and figured it out." I didn't hide the satisfaction in my voice.

"Something like that.... So what are you going to do now?" he asked.

"I think I need a shower and a margarita."

"Well, I meant in the long term, but a cold drink sounds good to me right now, too."

"In the long term? I'll keep doing what I'm doing now. I already have another case," I said proudly.

"Well, it looks like your first case was a success, but let's hope that your next case is a little less dramatic."

I ran my hand through my hair. "If it got any worse than this, I wouldn't know what to do."

"So why don't you let me buy you that margarita?" He flashed that sexy lopsided grin again.

The dimples appeared on his cheeks. Damn him.

"Well, I guess I could go for just one drink." I held up my index finger.

"Let me finish up here and I'll be ready." He pushed to his feet.

I nodded and smiled to myself as I watched him walk away.

Jake and I went to the little bar around the corner from my apartment. They made the tastiest and coldest margaritas that I'd ever had. Jake pulled out the stool for me as we sat at the bar. It felt strange to be sitting next to him in this social situation.

He ordered our drinks and turned to me. "It's about time you changed that sign on your office door, don't you think? You're in business for good now, right?"

I took a sip of my refreshing drink. "I think I'm officially a private eye now."

He held his glass up for a toast. "And a damn good one too."

Our eyes met and we looked at each other in silence for a long moment. I was pretty sure that I was blushing. I took a sip of my drink so that I wouldn't have to answer. I was at a loss for words.

We finished the drink and Jake walked me back to my apartment.

When I opened the door, Jake said, "Stay out of trouble, Thomas."

"Yeah, right." I watched Jake walk away and wondered if I'd ever see him again.

It turned out that Matt had hired the bodybuilders to intimidate me. He'd have killed me if that was what it took, though. Thank goodness it hadn't come to that.

Sam and Arthur had discovered Matt was taking money for bribes. The man who had followed me was someone Keith had hired. Matt had demanded that Chuck kill Arthur to repay Chuck's debt to Matt.

Matt Cooper had invested in the condos, but that wasn't the reason he'd killed Arthur and Thomas. He killed Arthur because Arthur was having an affair with Matt's wife. He'd had Thomas

killed because he was going to tell the police that Matt had killed Arthur.

Matt had been outraged that Arthur had been having an affair with his wife. So it was never about Arthur moving out of the condo after all, although that couldn't have helped the matter either. Allison had started her affair with Sam Louis to seek revenge against Arthur for his affair. It was tragic that it had come to that. Chuck Moore had confessed and Matt Cooper had been arrested. And thankfully Allison Abbott had been immediately released from jail.

Epilogue

The next day, I was sitting at my desk listening to Dorothy talk about the next Bunco game and her latest knitting project when Allison stopped by to thank me. She opened the door carrying a big bouquet of mixed flowers in shades of red, pink, and purple.

"They're beautiful," I said, taking the flowers from her. "But you didn't have to do that."

"You saved my life. Flowers don't seem like quite enough for something like that," she insisted.

"You hired me to find out who killed your husband and that's exactly what I did." I tried to hide my excitement so that I wouldn't seem completely unprofessional.

"You're good at your job," she said with a bright, wide smile.

With the case settled, I took the afternoon off. I'd picked up a red, blue, yellow, and white striped beach umbrella and a red and white polka-dotted beach chair at the shop across the street from the beach. Purely by accident, the beach chair matched my red and white polka-dotted bikini. I had also painted my toes a bright red to match the swimsuit. I'd probably dip my feet in the water, but I was still recovering from seeing Thomas Shaw's body washed up on shore. It would take a while to get that vision out of my head, if I ever did.

Maneuvering around the many tanning bodies, I found a good spot to set up camp. I set up the chair and umbrella on the warm

white sand, then slathered on my sunscreen. Grabbing my Kindle and cold drink, I settled down for a relaxing afternoon.

I had decided to take Dorothy's advice and stop and smell the ocean breeze once in a while. Ever since I'd taken over the agency, I'd been a bit obsessed with making the business successful. It had only been a week, but I felt I was off to a good start. But if I didn't stop to take a break once in a while, what was the point? There were quite a few people crowding the beach, but I'd planned on popping in my earbuds, cranking up the iPod, and tuning them out. A guy in a shiny blue Speedo winked as he walked by. I diverted my attention and pretended that I hadn't noticed.

I grabbed my beach tote and reached inside for my binoculars. I'd brought them so that I could look at the ships along the coast. I definitely wasn't going to check out the hot guys walking up and down the beach. Holding the binoculars up to my eyes, I scanned the coastline until I spotted a ship. It wasn't far from shore so I had a pretty good view of what was going on around the ship. I focused in on the gleaming white and blue vessel as it steadily moved across the water.

At first sight, the ship appeared to be empty. I moved my binoculars across its length. Movement finally caught my attention and I moved my snooping to the right just a tad. The binoculars almost fell out of my hands. I couldn't believe what I saw. A man led a woman across the deck. Well, he more or less dragged her. Her hands were bound behind her back and a blindfold covered her eyes. She had long black hair and wore a white bikini. The man was heavyset with dark hair. He wore a white shirt and dark blue shorts.

What the hell was going on? Had the man kidnapped the woman? What was he going to do to her? As the ship moved, I caught only a glimpse of the name on the stern. *Vita* was the last word, but what did the rest say? Unfortunately, I didn't have access

to a boat and couldn't save the woman on my own, so I had to call the police right away.

I threw my binoculars down and grabbed my phone.

"Mind if I join you?" The male voice drifted across the ocean air.

"What are you doing here?" I asked as I clutched my chest.

Jake's gaze raked over my exposed body. I suddenly felt naked in the polka-dotted bikini. It was like being out there in my underwear. Sunshine shimmered over his handsome face. He looked different in olive-green cargo shorts and a faded red T-shirt.

"I thought I'd drop by and say hello. Dorothy said you were on the beach. She actually brought me right out here to where you were." He looked over his shoulder and waved.

I looked back and saw Dorothy standing there with a huge smile on her face, waving at us. I'd get her for this later. I'd fill in her crossword puzzle with an ink pen. But there wasn't time to argue about Jake being there now. I had other things to worry about. Like the woman who was currently in danger.

Acknowledgments

To my son, who brings me joy every single day. To my mother, who introduced me to the love of books. To my husband, who encourages me and always has faith in me. A huge thank you to my editor, Meredith Giordan. And to the readers who make writing fun.

About the Author

Rose Pressey is a *USA Today*, Amazon, and Barnes & Noble Top 100 bestselling author. She enjoys writing quirky and fun novels with a paranormal twist. The paranormal has always captured her interest. The thought of finding answers to the unexplained fascinates her.

When she's not writing about werewolves, vampires, and every other supernatural creature, she loves eating cupcakes with sprinkles, reading, spending time with family, and listening to oldies from the fifties.

Rose suffers from Psoriatic Arthritis and has knee replacements. She might just set the world record for joint replacements. She's soon having her hips replaced.

Rose lives in the beautiful commonwealth of Kentucky with her husband, son, and three sassy Chihuahuas.

Visit her online at:
http://www.rosepressey.com
http://www.facebook.com/rosepressey
http://www.twitter.com/rosepressey

Rose loves to hear from readers. You can email her at rose@rosepressey.com.

If you're interested in receiving information when a new Rose Pressey book is released, you can sign up for her newsletter at www.rosepressey.com. Join her on Facebook for lots of fun and prizes.

Made in the USA
Lexington, KY
06 March 2014